The Girl They All Knew

Emma Tucker

Published by Emma Tucker, 2021.

The Girl They All Knew

Copyright 2021 Emma Tucker
Published by Emma Tucker

Chapter 1

Emily Green stepped off the DLR train. She was wearing a purple rockabilly dress, it was clenched in at the waist and flowed loosely around her knees, emanating the 1950s fashion except with little black skulls on its print. She made her way out of Lewisham train station, excited about the new year ahead in this part of London.

Walking down the street on this hot day in August, Emily enjoyed the bright weather. Shakira had said she would meet her just by the traffic lights, which were right next to the station. She had seen pictures of Shakira on her Facebook and had regarded her as pretty.

As Emily crossed the road and waved to Shakira, she felt a tingling sensation of nervousness. She had never met her before but she was good friends with Lisa, who would be renting the third room in their shared house.

Shakira was beautiful with dark deep-olive skin and long black hair. She had Hispanic looks; she was tall and very slender. She was wearing black boots and short shorts with tights underneath.

'Hi,' Emily said, greeting her new roommate who was also a fellow student at the University of Avenna.

'So, you're Emily. I guess we're going to be flatmates,' Shakira half-smiled.

They walked to the house on Grace Road. The property was tall and prestigious looking in the good part of town.

Shakira opened the door to the house and Emily followed her in. A huge mirror was mounted on the wall in the hallway, and Emily felt a sense of embarrassment as she saw her reflection.

She followed Shakira into the living room, which overlooked a moderately sized garden.

As Shakira handed Emily her keys to the house, her new roommate suggested they listen to some music and have a few beers.

Emily had never seen the house before, yet on the phone Lisa had described it as a nice property. It was very much a middle class house on a quiet street. The garden which overlooked the living room was well kept.

'What are you studying at Avenna?' Shakira said, handing Emily the cold beer.

'Fine art. What about you?'

'I'm a psychology student. I don't know why I chose it really. I guess because I got a C at the A-level.' Shakira opened her beer and took a large slug. 'Are you in your second year too?'

'Yeah. Second year, I met Lisa in halls. Were you in Shepherd House as well?'

'Nope. I was in Douglas. Did you go to many parties in your first year?'

'Not really,' Emily said as she looked down at the beer. 'I'm not the greatest partygoer.'

'Drink up!' Shakira smiled as she sat in the black sofa opposite where Emily was perched.

Emily hadn't drunk much for a while now. She remembered when she was a teenager how she and her best friend, Olivia, had loved to go out and have a few drinks. It had been a different era in Emily's life.

Shakira talked about herself. She explained how she wasn't sure if psychology was the right path for her, yet she wanted to finish her bachelor's degree.

As Emily drunk her beer, she described to Shakira how she had always been passionate about art. She explained how her half-brother also had a bachelor's in art and had gone on to get a master's degree.

'So, art runs in your family,' Shakira smiled as she went to the fridge to get them both another beer.

'I guess that's true.' Emily looked down at the floor, avoiding eye contact with Shakira. It was weird meeting this new girl and knowing that they were to live together.

By the time Shakira had finished her second beer, Emily had only finished her first.

'So where are you from originally?' Shakira asked.

'I lived in a town called Aylesbury. I hated it.'

'Why?'

Emily didn't want to talk about her past. She remembered the embarrassment of her psychotic episode, and how her peers had viewed her so differently after she became sick at the age of nineteen.

'It's just a boring, dull town,' Emily said. 'What about you, where are you from?'

'Originally I'm from Barcelona, but when I was ten, we moved to Fuengirola, which is an English ex-pat town. My parents moved there because it was cheap.'

'Oh, do you speak Spanish?'

'Si, tengo mucho de espanol, es mi lingua madre.' Shakira squinted her eyes as she looked at Emily. 'Tu mira no Buena. No bebe mucho alcohol?'

'Huh?' Emily stuttered, feeling a little queasy from the beer.

'You're not much of a drinker, are you?'

'Oh god! I think I'm going to be sick. Where's the toilet?' Emily squealed.

Shakira helped Emily to the downstairs bathroom. As Emily entered the bathroom and threw up in the toilet, she heard Shakira laughing quietly outside.

Emily cleaned her face up with some soap and water and then stepped out of the bathroom.

'I'm sorry about that,' she said.

'Man. It's OK. But seriously, one beer? Anyway, do you want me to show you to your bedroom?'

'Please.'

Emily followed Shakira upstairs to the middle bedroom. It was a large, square-shaped room. The bed was a single. There was a sink and a wardrobe inside the room.

'I'll let you unpack. Lisa will be here tomorrow,' smiled Shakira.

Emily opened up her suitcase and put her black laptop on the desk. She unpacked her rockabilly clothes and put her summer jackets in the wardrobe; her clothes were inspired by an alternative, somewhat gothic sense in fashion.

New blankets and sheets were still in their Argos packaging waiting for her to use them. She made her fresh bed, ready for sleep later that night.

Emily thought about how she had been a bit lonely in her first year. A few of the girls in her halls had been nice, but she hadn't known how to make a lasting friendship. The ones that were louder and more outgoing had seemed to stick together.

Most weekends Emily had gone back to Aylesbury where she would spend time with her friend Craig. They would order takeaways and watch horror movies.

Shakira had left a card with the Wi-Fi password on the empty desk. Emily sat on the little tub stool and set up the Wi-Fi on her laptop. She saw on Facebook that Olivia was partying in a fancy club. There were glamorous pictures of Olivia with her slender, shiny friends. Emily felt a weird sensation of wanting to be slim like Olivia was. She felt that was one of the reasons they had become friends when they were teenagers because of their shared beauty.

Emily had met Olivia when she was seventeen and in her first year of her BTEC in art. Olivia had left a local private school in Aylesbury. She had come to Aylesbury College where Emily studied to retake her GCSEs. Olivia had made contact with Emily on Myspace, saying how she had noticed her in college due to her unique and stylish fashion taste.

They had probably become such good friends because they were both beautiful misfits. Neither of them had done too great academically so far. Olivia hadn't been able to cope at private school and flunked her GCSEs. Emily had to do a foundation diploma before being allowed onto the BTEC course, which she was studying the year she met Olivia.

More people had come into Emily's life during the years she was close friends with Olivia. She had become popular, getting acquainted with many local teenagers.

Yet when she went crazy and developed a mental illness, everyone thought she was barking mad.

Yet that was behind her. She didn't like to think about the psychiatric ward. She always did her best to push those horrible thoughts out of her mind. Emily felt as though life would feel so different if she had never got sick.

***

The next day Lisa arrived at the house with her father, who had given her a lift to Lewisham. They were standing outside, leaning against his white car. Lisa's father was shorter than her and appeared to be a very quiet man in the way he simply nodded when greeted by Shakira and Emily.

Lisa's hair was bright green this year. Last year it had been purple. She had a butterfly in her hair and was wearing a stripey dress and plimsolls that revealed the tattoos on her feet.

Shakira stepped outside, while Emily joined them outside the house. Shakira embraced Lisa with a hug.

'So good to have you here,' Shakira beamed.

'Shakira! Your hug is a little bit bear-like.'

'Oh, sorry,' Shakira said, and stepped back into the house.

As Lisa and her father carried her suitcases inside, Shakira showed them to her bedroom which would be the largest in the house, because Lisa was sharing it with her boyfriend from Dublin called Aiden.

'Aiden's just doing a few more recordings with the band before they split for good,' Lisa said. 'He'll be here by the end of the month.'

Lisa's father helped her unpack. She had a lot of interesting stuff. Her wardrobe was full of bizarre clothing items. She placed abstract art on the walls.

'No not there, Dad – put it here,' Lisa barked at her father.

'Sorry, love,' he mumbled.

After two hours had passed, all of Lisa's stuff was unpacked and her father was ready to drive back to Hammersmith where he lived.

Emily knew how Lisa's parents were both property developers and had offered to buy her a property for her second year at university. Lisa had told her all this and how she had felt that living with friends would be better for her. The two girls had been excited to rent together. Lisa had expressed how she wanted Shakira to be the final tenant in the house with them.

Emily had really gelled with Lisa during halls of residence. She had only gone out with her once during their first year of university, yet they had bonded through talking on Facebook.

Lisa was studying graphic design and was one of the prettiest girls at university in Emily's opinion. She was so tall, and had a unique sense of fashion, yet she was also bossy and obsessed with her boyfriend, Aiden, who she had met at a gig during their first term at university.

Emily had seen pictures of Aiden on Lisa's Facebook.

As the evening became night, the three girls ordered sushi from a local takeaway. They sat in the living room eating their boxes of sushi and rice.

Emily felt a little shy around Shakira; she found she had a loud, confident aura which made her feel uneasy. It was a quality she wouldn't have even noticed once, yet nowadays she was more anxious around loud people.

'Let's go out tomorrow,' announced Shakira.

'Where to?' Lisa said.

'There's a few really good bars locally. Perhaps we could go to the Dirty South tomorrow night.'

The girls agreed that they would go out tomorrow night.

***

Emily dressed in a black boofy dress which had a huge, flared design, with a red cardigan with a knitted dog embroidered on its side. Her black hair was frazzled from the bleach that she had applied herself the previous summer, yet she had coloured it black. Yet the condition of her hair wasn't the best.

As she stepped out of her room and greeted Shakira and Lisa, she was aware of how she felt so fat in comparison to them.

She remembered when she and Olivia would go out. They had both been a dress size eight, yet Emily was taller. Both girls had looked like fashion models and attracted a lot of attention. She felt bad about herself as she remembered who she used to be and who she had become.

'You look nice.' Lisa smiled at Emily.

Lisa was wearing a red pencil dress, a fake leather jacket and small black heels, and she looked gorgeous. Her green hair was tied up in a bun with a purple flower at the side.

The three girls made their way to the Dirty South. It was a short walk from the house. The pub was quiet, as it was a Sunday, but students were occupying some of the tables. The nearest university to Lewisham was Goldsmith, yet the three girls attended the University of Avenna.

The girls ordered their first round of drinks. Emily felt a hot sense of shyness as they posed for a selfie. She found it hard to smile in the picture, feeling worried about having a double chin. She endured intense feelings about how fat she looked in the picture as she looked at the photo Shakira had taken on her mobile phone.

As the night progressed and a live band played a rough and melodic rock performance, Emily started to feel at ease. She started to feel more comfortable with Shakira, who, although a little loud, was obviously a genuinely nice girl.

By the time the pub was preparing to close, the three girls stepped out and walked home hand in hand singing, '*I love you baby, and if it's quite all right, I need you, baby.*'

As they unlinked and laughed to themselves, Lisa suggested they get some chips. They made their way to the kebab shop, where a woman with a silver wig walked by and violently knocked into Emily.

Emily steadied her balance as the woman who was talking to herself passed them.

'Idiot!' shouted Shakira in the direction of the woman with the wig.

'Are you all right?' Lisa asked.

'Yeah. I'm fine,' smiled Emily.

The three girls bought chips and cola from the kebab shop. They took their food home and ate their meal in the living room.

Emily went to bed happy that night. She was happy that she would be living with Shakira and Lisa for the duration of her second year. Perhaps they'd continue to share a house in her third year. She hoped that Lisa's boyfriend would be easy to get along with.

Yet as Emily applied oil to her dry hair and took off her makeup, she remembered the woman with the silver wig. She saw a weird image of her mad brown eyes in her mind and wondered why she would think of such a thing when she had never seen the woman's face.

When her face was bare of makeup, she changed into Disney pyjamas and got into her warm bed. That night in her dreams there was laughter and a strange sense of energy that she didn't understand.

Emily bolted upright in the morning when her little Samsung phone alarm rang. It was an ordinary Monday, but she felt a strange sensation that something had changed in her – yet what? Why was she feeling so strange?

Chapter 2

Emily felt a sense of hope in the air. It was the summer before her second year of university and she was excited for all the world had to offer her.

Shakira was preparing herself a coffee when Emily came downstairs.

'Morning,' Shakira smiled; her long black hair was unbrushed yet sleek.

Emily thought to herself how she would like a coffee. As she thought this thought, Shakira instantly got her mug from the kitchen and began making her one.

'You'd like a coffee, right?' Shakira smiled brightly.

'Sure,' Emily said.

The girls sat down on the black sofa with their coffees. Emily thought how she should make some toast and a weird thought popped into her head. What if Shakira made her toast?

Shakira hopped up from the sofa, placing her coffee on the table. 'I'm going to make us both some toast.'

Emily thought about how that was odd. It wasn't until later on that day when Emily thought about how she needed to go shopping and Shakira said they both needed new clothes, that Emily felt a strange sense of curiosity. Shakira suggested that they go to Primark.

Shakira was wearing a pair of skinny black jeans and a loose-fitting green shirt; she looked model-like. Emily thought to herself how nice it would be if Shakira got her something from Primark.

'You know what,' Shakira smiled, picking up a pair of size sixteen skinny jeans from the rail, 'these would look banging on your curvy figure.'

Emily smiled as she put the jeans in her shopping basket. 'Do you really think so?'

'Curvy girls look great in these type of jeans. I'll even buy them for you,' Shakira said.

Emily tried on the jeans, which fitted perfectly. They weren't something she would normally wear. Yet it was so odd how Shakira had suggested to buy them after Emily thought the thought.

She tested her weird suspicion once more when she looked at a cheap pair of fuzzy socks. Shakira instantly picked them up and purchased them for Emily. Something weird was afoot. What on Earth was going on?

When they got home, Emily went upstairs and put the jeans in her chest of drawers.

Over the next week Emily spent time with Shakira and Lisa. Once they went to the cinema and had a meal in Greenwich. Another time they visited 286, which Emily thought was a really good karaoke bar in Lewisham. Emily thought Lisa had an averagely pleasant singing voice. Its thin and raspy sound was accentuated by her regular smoking habit. Emily herself didn't smoke, she noticed how a lot of the girls she had known in her life were smokers.

A few days later, Emily was sitting in the living room with Shakira and Lisa.

Shakira was looking for a part-time job on her laptop. She had told her flatmates that she was planning to work on the weekends.

'What sort of job do you want?' Lisa asked.

'I was thinking about bar work or something in retail,' Shakira said.

The girls agreed that it was a good idea for Shakira to get a part-time job. Her family were not rich. Her mother was a receptionist and her father was unemployed. They were living in Spain and Shakira would not see them until Christmas time.

Emily was also on her laptop. She received an email and her face felt flushed with hot embarrassment.

'What are you looking at on there?' Shakira smirked.

'It's a dating site. Someone I have been talking to for a few days asked me if we should meet in person. I think I might delete my account though, as I need to concentrate on my studies,' Emily said.

'For goodness sake. It's not like you have a heavy subject like I do,' smirked Shakira. 'Art's one of the easy subjects. Let's see what this mysterious man looks like.'

Emily showed Shakira and Lisa the profile picture of Parker, who had asked her on a date tonight.

'He's very hot,' said Lisa. 'If he's interested, you should give him a chance of a date, sparks might fly.'

'I guess,' Emily said as she replied to Parker, stating that she would agree to go on a date.

'At it, girl. Now all I need to do is find myself a hot boyfriend,' Shakira said.

Shakira cooked the girls a nice dinner. She made oven cooked chicken with mash and veg. Emily did not really cook much for herself; she was embarrassed to admit her dad had been a professional chef yet she had never taken much of an interest in cooking.

After the meal, the girls chatted about this and that. They were all excited about their second-year studies at the University of Avenna.

When Emily returned to her room, she looked at Parker's profile again. He was indeed very good looking, with brown hair and a slim body. In her conversations with him during the week, he sounded kind and educated. He said he was looking for something serious.

Emily's last relationship had been two years ago, before she got ill. She had been eighteen and in her final year of a BTEC in art at Aylesbury College. It had been a strange year. She had felt alone while dating, since her heart had not been in the relationship. He had been twenty-four years old. Her dad had not approved of the relationship because he thought he was too old for her.

Emily felt anxious at the thought of meeting Parker. She knew in her heart that if she were still slim, she would have been excited about meeting him. Yet Emily was riddled with insecurity with her body. She was between a size fourteen to sixteen and was sure she was putting on more weight.

He was a journalism graduate and seemed like someone interesting from the various places where the several pictures on his dating profile were taken.

Yet dating frightened her now and intimacy filled her with terror. She did not like to dwell on these thoughts.

***

A few days passed, before Emily was to meet Parker. He lived quite near to her, and he worked in a local bank.

They met in Lewisham, which was the town in South London where Emily was renting with her friends. Lewisham was close to Greenwich, where Parker lived. Emily wore a navy-blue dress and black cardigan, she thought that the clothes were elegant yet she longed for a slimmer body. Her flatmates had straightened her hair and applied clip-in hair extensions, which made her hair look long and pretty.

Parker hugged her when they met. He was about 5 foot 10 and smelled of cologne. Emily thought he looked sharp. He did not have any visible tattoos or piercings, unlike Emily who had a piercing above her lip and the left side of her nose. It was hard to read Parker's expression and tell whether he was attracted to her or not.

'It's good to meet you in person,' he said.

'Likewise.'

Parker and Emily were standing outside Lewisham train station. He suggested that they go to a restaurant for a meal. They decided upon Nando's which was a short walk into the town centre.

'So, tell me a little more about yourself,' Parker said when they sat in Nando's.

'Well... as you know, I'm studying art at Avenna. I love dogs. My parents have two dogs back home,' Emily said.

'Cool. What are their names?'

'Misty and Sasha.'

'That's great,' Parker said, smiling with a dull, uninterested expression as he ate his meal and talked with her.

Emily was feeling that something was missing from their interaction.

'I think we could be good friends. If that's all right with you?' Parker said, smiling in a kindly manner.

Emily had expected him to say that. She felt he probably wouldn't have wanted to be just friends if she was still a size eight. Yet she understood and was relieved in many respects.

She could feel how the chemistry between them was not right. She could feel his lack of attraction in the way he smiled at her. It was as though there was no electricity in the air between her. Emily remembered times when she had met boys in her teens and the air had felt buzzing with chemistry.

'It would be nice to be friends,' Emily said.

'I really mean that... You are not my type, and please don't think it doesn't mean I don't think you're cute. I do. It's just you're not what I'm looking for.'

After the meal, Emily stood outside Nando's with Parker. They wished each other farewell as they parted ways as Parker made his way to the train station.

Emily walked home. She knew it was not a healthy thing to be feeling. Yet romance did not seem to belong to her, not when she had gained this weight, that made her feel like she was waiting to re-blossom into the beautiful young woman she had been in her teenage years. The girl that was always being asked out on dates.

When she got home, Shakira was in but Lisa had gone out to visit her parents.

'How did the date go?' asked Shakira.

'He just wanted to be friends.'

'No casual sex then?' Shakira said, raising an eyebrow.

'It's not my kind of thing, casual sex, and no, he just wanted to be platonic friends.'

'Shame. Well, keep looking. When we go back to uni in September you might meet a hot guy there.'

'Maybe,' sighed Emily. 'So, what have you been up to?'

'Well I only went and got myself a job interview for a swanky pub in Holborn.'

'That's great,' Emily said.

Shakira went to hug Emily, to her surprise. She smelt of cigarettes and floral perfume.

As Emily talked with Shakira, she thought how girls like her were more confident with men. Shakira told her how she had slept with two guys during her first year at university.

Emily had met a cute guy at a club called Sinn in Camden during her first year, yet she had not given him a chance. She had been too consumed with insecurity to allow herself to date.

She thought about Parker. He had seemed like a really nice guy and she respected his decision to only want to be friends.

Yet as she thought this, a weird intrusive thought in her mind said, 'What if he liked you?' As she imagined him looking at her with those chocolate eyes and slender cheeks, she envisioned him at the restaurant explaining how he really liked her. She imagined a whole alternate tale of events where he had asked her to be his girlfriend.

'So, do you fancy a takeaway for dinner tonight?' asked Shakira.

'Sure,' Emily replied.

Emily's phone began to buzz. It was Parker. She felt her hands shake as she answered the call.

'Hi Parker, is everything OK?' Emily said as she put the call on loudspeaker.

'I don't know why I said I wasn't interested in you, Emily. I think I was feeling shy... I am not usually shy, you know. I don't know what I'm saying because it's so weird... it's like BAM , my feelings for you have just sort of blossomed.'

'Weird,' mouthed Shakira as she listened to the phone call.

'I don't know. Maybe it is best we're just friends,' Emily said.

'Give him a chance... he's a hottie,' whispered Shakira.

'Please. Give me just one more chance, we only just met. These things aren't easy for guys either. It's like a switch just turned on in my brain. I am seeing you again in my mind... God... I'm sorry... I just really want to try things out with you.' Parker sounded upset.

'I guess we could go on another date. Maybe Sunday?' Emily said, feeling weird about the whole situation. It was his choice of words... how a switch had been turned on in his brain.

'You won't regret this. I'll text you later, OK,' Parker said, then hung up the phone.

Shakira squealed with delight. 'He was just shy by the sounds of it.'

'I guess,' Emily said, thinking about the strange woman they had bumped into the other night only two weeks ago. Things just did not seem the same. It was like something magical was buzzing in the air and it was a little creepy. Emily remembered how after that night it was like something had changed in her. That was the moment when things had become a little creepy and coincidences seemed too odd.

Shakira and Emily were getting on really well. She felt as though they would have many more fun times in the house together. Emily was starting to feel comfortable in Shakira's presence.

'I should tell you something... about me...' Emily said as they sat in the living room together.

'What?' Shakira said.

'I've got a mental illness called bipolar affective disorder.'

'Oh yeah. Lisa already told me about that. How you were sectioned when you lived in Aylesbury. Yeah, it's OK. You don't need to talk about it if you don't want to. I've known people back in Fuengirola who had mental health issues.'

'Thanks for being understanding,' Emily said, feeling relieved that Shakira hadn't made a big deal out of what she just told her.

'I have things about Fuengirola I don't like to remember, you know? I was really unhappy in high school. I hate to think about it.'

They changed the subject as they waited for the Domino's pizzas to be delivered.

'Will you do my hair nice again when I next see Parker?' Emily said.

'Well, of course. We have to make sure you look lovely when you see him. Give the guy another chance. I really think things between you and him could go well,' Shakira said.

'I was thinking of wearing a rockabilly dress when I see Parker again.'

Shakira agreed that would be a good idea. The girls excitedly chatted about Emily seeing Parker again. Shakira couldn't see the inner concern that Emily had about meeting with Parker, how it filled her with internal anxiety. Emily was glad when the pizza arrived and they changed their conversation topic.

***

On Sunday afternoon Emily waited for Parker outside Prezzo, which was an Italian chain restaurant. She had the same hair extensions, along with chunky red earrings and bright lipstick. She felt that she had made the best of herself in what she was wearing.

'You look great,' Parker said as he greeted her. He was dressed incredible sharp. Parker was wearing a crisp white shirt and black jeans, and the leather jacket he wore looked like it might be designer. He handed her a bouquet of red roses. 'Here, these are for you.'

'Thank you,' said Emily, blushing.

Inside the restaurant, Parker said she could have whatever she wanted and the bill was on him.

'So, how has your week been?' Emily said.

'Oh, it's been busy. Work's good. I've been watching a few documentaries and thinking about writing a novel.'

'Oh wow. You want to write a novel?'

'Well yeah. I studied journalism as a way to become a writer. I keep a blog where I write about society and travel. It's had over a thousand hits in the last month.' Parker's voice lit up. 'I might even write you into my novel.'

'I'm not interesting enough to be in a book,' Emily replied, thinking how something was not quite right. It was the enthusiasm in his voice, which had not been there on their first date.

Emily learned that Parker was originally from Laugharne, a quiet village in Wales. He loved it there but had wanted the busy London life during his studies at university.

'I'd like to see you again,' Parker said as the dessert menu arrived.

Emily did not know if she wanted to see Parker again. Sure, he was beautiful and kind, yet his interaction with her felt forced. It was actually rather spooky, as if something was motivating him that was unnatural.

Yet Emily also knew that she wanted to impress Shakira and Lisa and friends like Olivia. She wanted them to think that she was doing well. She wanted to believe in the story she spun. She wanted to approve of her budding relationship and see her as being something like the girl she remembered being before her illness. The girl who dated and was confident.

'Sure, I'd like that,' Emily said, even though she felt a sense of dread at the idea of a third date with Parker.

After the meal they agreed that next week they would go to a restaurant he recommended in Soho. He said he loved the Chinese food at this place and they could go for a few drinks afterwards.

***

A few days passed where every day Parker would text her. He began texting her little verses of poetry which described her beauty; it felt too much too soon.

As the days led up to their third date, Emily tried to think positively about the new budding relationship; maybe she was just being paranoid because it had been a long time since she'd had a boyfriend.

On the day that Aiden moved in, Emily felt a cold sensation of social awkwardness in the air. Emily had seen many photos of Aiden on Lisa's Facebook. He was six foot, tall and skinny, with long hair, one side was coloured blond and the other side black. He had tattoos all over his visible torso and neck.

Lisa flung her arms around him when he entered the house. Emily sensed he had a cold energy to him. It was strange how Emily felt she could sense the fact he wasn't a very nice person in his aura. Yet she could also feel a sense of how he did indeed love Lisa very much; it was as though it radiated from him.

'Oh my, it's so good to have you home,' Lisa said, and then she passionately kissed Aiden.

'I'm glad to be at my new home, my lovely,' Aiden said.

Aiden unpacked his belongings in Lisa's room. They shared the biggest bedroom in the house. He left his guitar in the hallway.

'Just a heads up,' whispered Shakira when Aiden and Lisa were upstairs, 'Aiden can be a bit of a prick.'

'Oh, OK,' whispered Emily, feeling concerned.

There was something unfriendly in his aura, yet why could Emily sense this? She had never sensed emotions and personalities off people before. It had begun on the second date with Parker, when she noticed how she could feel his kindness, yet she knew something was wrong inside of him. It was like a force was working against him.

That night, when Emily prepared for bed, she looked at the photographs she had taken on her phone from the afternoon of her second date with Parker. A lot of people, including guys, had liked the pictures on her Facebook. Even Olivia had liked the photographs.

She looked at herself in the images and felt a smile break across her face. She looked gorgeous in the pictures. Yet it was hard for her to love herself when she wore mostly size fourteen or sixteen clothes, as she had recently gained weight since moving into the house.

She remembered when she had been a pre-teen, how she had told herself she would not let herself be fully happy unless she was thin. She wondered what her fourteen-year-old self would think if she was her now, aged twenty-two and overweight. Would her younger self be disgusted at who she had become?

Emily did her best to think about all she had achieved. She had done really well in her BTEC when she was a teenager. She was on the road to getting a good degree from the University of Avenna. She loved art with a passion, it made her heart sing with joy.

Emily decided to be happy with the way things were tonight. Life was not perfect, yet things weren't too bad either.

Chapter 3

Emily couldn't stop thinking about how odd the coincidences were, it was niggling at her. As she prepared for her third date with Parker, she felt uneasy.

She looked in the mirror at the chubby girl who had gained four pounds since her last date with him only a week ago. Who was she fooling? Parker was the type of guy she would have dated before she became this person; she would have gone out with him in a heartbeat. Emily felt like a different human being from the slim girl who had not yet experienced a mental illness that would require her to take several tablets a day. Yet now, she didn't think that she was his type. Her thoughts were angrily telling her to cancel the date.

Yet she wanted to be like Shakira who was so confident with men, or Lisa who seemed so in love with Aiden.

Emily walked to the train station where she was to meet Parker. The weather was starting to get a little colder and the air felt crisp and bitter.

When she arrived, he was dressed in blue jeans and a leather jacket, he looked like a fashion model. The sunlight of the mid-morning showed just how gorgeous he was.

They boarded the train en route to Soho in central London.

'How's that novel going?' Emily asked.

'Good,' Parker said, blushing ever so slightly. 'Actually, I've decided to add a character inspired by you as a love interest, I hope you don't mind. I've called the character Esme.'

Emily felt her stomach tighten as she continued to wonder where this intensity from Parker was coming from. Even when she had been "beautiful" guys had always played it cool with her.

'That's great. I'm sure the novel will be amazing and I can't wait to read it one day,' Emily said, hiding the fact that she was a little freaked out by Parker's over-enthusiasm.

Parker talked about how it was his first attempt at novel writing. Emily talked about how she was looking forward to going back to her studies at Avenna.

By the time they arrived, Emily had learnt that Parker had been in a serious relationship a year ago, which had lasted six years. Emily wondered if he still loved his ex-girlfriend.

Soho was full of colourful buildings and bustling bars. The properties in this part of London were exclusive and for the rich alone; yet the bars were full of young people infused with alcohol. These young people frequenting Soho were brightly decorated in modern fashions. Some of the young couples Emily noticed were goths with tattoos and piercings.

Parker took her to the Chinese restaurant, which was fairly packed, yet he had booked a table. It was a cheap buffet restaurant yet he said it did the best Chinese food in London.

'I really like you,' Parker said as he gazed into her eyes with a strange intensity.

'I like you as well,' Emily quickly replied, feeling unsure if that was really true.

'I think we have something special,' Parker said.

'Sure,' Emily replied, smiling.

Parker described a creative writing group he had joined at university, and how everyone had told him his idea was unoriginal.

'They all told me I should write something else,' Parker said. 'But I've been told there's no such thing as original ideas, not truly.'

After the meal, they went to a bar called The Black Panther. It was small and dimly lit and smelt heavily of alcohol. The bar sold alcohol-pops and beers. The twenty-somethings there looked pretty and thin. The girl at the bar gave Parker a questioning look as she eyed him up with Emily.

Emily had a glass of wine and Parker drank a beer.

'You should pick where we go on our next date,' Parker said.

Emily imagined where she would want to go with Parker. Somewhere where people wouldn't notice how the couple looked unnatural.

As she thought this, she saw the kindness in his eyes and felt guilty for her negative thoughts.

'When I was a teenager I was very slim, I looked more like the kind of girl you'd be dating back then.'

Parker sighed. 'Emily, I'm here with you now.'

Parker leaned over to kiss her. It was the first time they had kissed, his breath was minty fresh and his skin was cool against her touch. Emily felt her heartbeat in her chest and could hear someone nearby laughing quietly; she wondered if it was at her.

'I can't wait for our next date,' Parker said as they left the bar. They travelled back to the train station to South London. Throughout the journey Parker held Emily's hand and once or twice kissed her gently on the cheek.

When it was time for them to part, Parker kissed her once more with passion outside of Lewisham train station.

'See you again soon,' Emily said as she let go of his hand and watched him walk back into the train station. She felt the anxiety buzz inside of her.

***

When Emily got home that evening, everyone was there. Shakira was in the living room drinking coffee, and Aiden and Lisa were in their room. Shakira looked at her with a curious and excited expression.

'Tell me everything about the date!'

'It was OK. He's a lovely guy. I guess I like him.'

'So... do you think you'll get serious?' Shakira asked.

'I don't know, I guess.'

'Well, you've been on three dates already. You know, three's the magic number usually for the birds and the bees if you know what I mean,' Shakira said with a laugh.

'I'm not sure.' Emily wanted to talk with Shakira about how things didn't feel right with Parker, yet she didn't feel that her friend would understand.

'He's really hot, live a little, you're twenty-two for goodness sake. You don't want to become a nun or a crazy cat lady, well, dog lady in your case. Yes your dogs at your parents' house are adorable, we've all seen the pictures.'

'I guess not,' Emily said. She would feel safer as a crazy old dog lady than sleeping with Parker or with various men the way Shakira did.

Emily didn't know what to think of Parker, something was missing. It did feel as though something was off and she couldn't brush off the feeling, yet surely it was illogical.

As Emily was about to change the subject, Aiden came downstairs.

'How'd the date go with Mr Handsome?' said Aiden.

'It was OK,' Emily said quietly.

'I was just telling her how she needs to give it up soon or he'll lose interest, the way you men do,' Shakira said to Aiden.

'Certainly. The only way she'll keep him is if she lets him have a go,' Aiden said with a cold look.

Emily felt embarrassed by his comments. She felt hurt but she also felt it was kind of true.

'Lisa wants to go to the Fox and Firkin tonight, you two are invited,' Aiden said.

'I can't go, I've got work,' said Shakira.

'Well, that just leaves you then,' sighed Aiden as he looked at Emily.

'I'd like to go,' Emily said.

She'd never been to that pub but had heard such good things about it.

***

Emily returned to her room after taking a quick shower and changed into some jeans and a black System of a Down band T-shirt. She applied Dior perfume to her neck and arms. She was a bit drained by the date with Parker and his eager texting. She felt pressurized by the poetic language he used, which seemed just way too much. *Your beauty mesmerised me today. My fallen angel,'* read one of Parker's poetic texts.

When she went downstairs to leave the house with Aiden and Lisa, she thought how good they looked. Lisa was so stunning with her green hair and long, black, velvet dress. She seemed like she was ready for Halloween.

The Fox and Firkin was a fifteen-minute walk from the house. The night was cool and the air felt good. The three of them didn't talk much of their way to the pub.

Inside it was fairly quiet. Rockabilly gothic, patterned curtains covered the windows and the pub walls were coloured a deep purple. Emily instantly took a liking to the pub, feeling as though it had a fairly relaxed atmosphere.

They sat near the entrance, where they could see the band that would play from afar. Aiden went up and got them all cocktails.

'So, are you happy with Parker?' Lisa asked.

'I think so.'

'Well, you should have a fair idea by now.'

'I guess. I know this is weird, but something feels off about dating Parker. It's like he's not being himself and something strange is controlling his actions. There, I said it.'

Lisa gave her a quizzical look. 'You're being paranoid. If you like him, I'm sure things will work out well.'

Aiden arrived back with the drinks. He kissed Lisa on the cheek and sat down. The group talked about how the girls would all be starting back at the University of Avenna next week. Aiden was looking for work as he was not a university student.

As the group chatted, the band began to play; they were young men in their twenties, and they gave an energetic performance. Emily enjoyed listening to them. She drank two cocktail drinks that night which were infused with fruit and vodka, and both her and Lisa agreed that the drinks were very nice at the pub. Emily soon stopped worrying about her new relationship with Parker. She was pleased to be forgetting about her worries and enjoying herself.

As she made her way to the toilets, a black guy with bleached blond hair approached her. He was very good looking due to his slender yet muscular physique. His facial features were finely carved.

'Hi,' said the guy.

'Errr hi,' Emily said.

'Come and talk with me outside in the beer garden,' said the man, and he looked into Emily's eyes with such power it was like a wave of compulsion washed over her.

'Of course,' Emily said, feeling the pull of his request as she followed him into the empty beer garden.

'Do not fear me,' he said as he looked into her eyes, pulling her into his gaze.

'I won't fear you,' echoed Emily.

'I know what you've become, and I am asking you not to be afraid but obey.'

'Yes.'

'My name is Kordell and I am a vampire; that's why I could sense what you've become. Someone must have passed on their ability to be a Destiny Walker to you.'

Emily didn't say anything, as the vampire's compulsion stopped her feeling fear at this revelation. Yet she had so many questions that she wanted to ask Kordell. So many vital things she desperately wanted to know.

'I want you to trust me so that I don't have to completely compel you. You won't tell anyone what you are and you will not reveal my identity,' Kordell said.

'Of course.'

They exchanged phone numbers and Kordell's eyes seemed to flash blue from brown in a moment.

'I'm not one of the bad guys. I do not kill people or do anything of the evil kind.'

'When did I become a Destiny Walker?'

'I don't know. I can help you find out, though,' Kordell said. 'Go back to your friends and play it cool. I'll call you tonight and we can meet again soon. We can figure out why this happened to you and work out a plan of action. I guess you haven't fully come into your powers yet, I can feel that off you.'

'Oh, OK,' Emily said, feeling a wealth of anxious worries as she remembered the last few weeks and all the weird coincidences. Thoughts of Parker and how unnatural he seemed raced through her mind, and the idea of becoming a supernatural being filled her with horror.

The idea that there were vampires in the world scared her, normality seemed to be crumbling around her.

Emily went back to her friends and watched as Kordell made his way out of the pub and waved at her as he left.

'Who was that?' Lisa said.

'That was my friend from uni,' Emily lied.

'Does he live locally?' Lisa said.

'I'm not sure. We don't know each other that well.'

The rest of the night seemed to wash over Emily. She did her best to listen to Lisa and Aiden but she kept missing out what they were talking about, because her mind was on the meeting with Kordell.

'You're being more odd than usual,' Lisa remarked just before they left to go home when the pub was about to close.

Emily thought to herself how people often described her as quirky and having a particularly unique personality. Yet now she was truly different.

***

That night, when Emily got home, she looked at her phone to see a text from Kordell saying that he would call on her tonight and that she was to leave her window open. She wanted to fight the urge to do so, yet she was still under his compulsion.

As she left the window open as wide as possible, her hands were shaking. Was Kordell one of the good guys, or would she die tonight at the hands of a vampire?

Emily waited. She looked at her phone and saw it was almost one in the morning. Everyone was asleep and the house was quiet. Half an hour later, Kordell slipped into the room as quickly as a cat and stood by the window.

'Hi,' he whispered. 'I will explain everything.'

Kordell explained that a Destiny Walker was someone with the power to alter people's fate by their desire. He explained it was a dangerous power to have, and that many people with this ability had lived terrible lives.

'It can be passed on to another, though, that's obviously what happened to you,' Kordell said.

Emily was frightened by the prospect of her power. She was scared of Kordell and the way his eyes quickly changed from brown to blue and how he had flashed his fangs to prove he was a vampire and his skin had become all veiny when he did this.

'You promise you won't hurt me?' Emily said.

'I promise. I assure you that I'm one of the good guys. I was turned in the 1950s against my will. I never wanted this life, just the way you didn't want to become a Destiny Walker.'

Emily thought of Parker, of how he had seemed forced and unnatural around her. She was scared to tell Kordell about him yet felt she needed some advice.

'The guy I've been on three dates with seems weird. It's like something is forcing his actions. Do you think maybe I influenced him with my will as you described?'

'Quite possibly.' Kordell looked at her with a curious expression. 'Try to imagine breaking that link. Will it in your heart that any magic upon this guy will be broken.'

'I'll try,' Emily said as she envisioned Parker in her mind's eye. She imagined the magic that might be influencing him as if it was a golden rope around his neck. In her mind she cut the rope and imagined it falling to the floor.

Kordell explained to Emily how magical beings frequented the world. There were witches and werewolves amongst them, even fairies existed but they were not little creatures like the fairy tale books described them.

'I'll call you soon and we can discuss an action plan; we can try and work out if you want to pass on your powers or learn to control them,' said Kordell.

Kordell slipped out of the window. Emily closed the window, as the night air had made her room cold. She hoped she could trust Kordell; she believed he was telling her the truth.

She spent the rest of the night online watching music videos on YouTube. By the time it was six in the morning she was exhausted and crawled into bed.

***

Emily awoke at three in the afternoon to see two missed calls from Parker and a voice message.

'Emily, I... I don't know how to say this but I don't think we are right for each other. I am so sorry because I've messed you around and I don't want to hurt you. I think it's best if we don't see each other again. I'm sorry,' said the voice message.

She felt a little sad to think that she must have influenced him in the first place to want to date her. It felt horrible to think she had worked magic over him. It was horrifying to contemplate how he might have continued to have false feelings for her if she had never met Kordell and learnt the truth.

It was a relief to know she wouldn't see Parker again. She didn't know what she was going to do about her powers, but at least that was one less stressful thing to deal with. She hadn't been comfortable with Parker. She hoped he would find someone he genuinely connected with, and she wished the same thing for herself.

Chapter 4

Three years before Emily moved into the shared house in Lewisham, where she was about to start her second year of university at Avenna, the year was 2008. Emily had just finished her BTEC in fine art at Aylesbury College. It was a warm July and Emily was waiting for her exam results.

She was feeling confident that she had done well. Her art teacher had said she was one of the best students in the class.

As she straightened her black hair and applied hair extensions, she thought about how college was now over and a new chapter in her life lay before her. She imagined what the boys at university would think of her, imagining they would be interested in her because of her pretty looks.

Emily was wearing a size eight leopard-print pair of pyjamas, which she had purchased in the Black Rose boutique in Camden. She felt slim and sexy in her body, which the clothes in her wardrobe highlighted. She felt powerful because of her beauty.

Her best friend, Olivia, who was a year younger than her, was visiting her house tonight. They had met at college when Emily was in her first year of the BTEC and Olivia was retaking her GCSEs.

Emily opened up her pink Nokia flip phone and took a photo. She knew she was indeed a stunning girl.

Her mum knocked. 'Emily, what time is Olivia getting here?' As she entered, both the dogs came rushing into Emily's room.

'In a few minutes,' Emily said.

Emily cuddled her dogs as her mother stood in the entrance of her room. The bedroom was painted a hot pink colour and had pages from fashion magazines stuck to the wall. Some of Emily's artwork hung on the wall too. Emily's art was bold images of people in vivid colours. Emily liked how her room illustrated her personality and artistic talent so much.

'It's good that you have a best friend like Olivia. She's a really nice girl,' her mother said.

'Olivia's a good pal.'

'I'm so proud of you for finishing college. I know it's not easy for young girls growing up, and you've achieved so much,' her mum said.

'Mum! Don't embarrass me in front of the dogs,' laughed Emily.

'They don't mind. I'll let you get ready in peace.'

Emily nodded and her mother left her room. The two dogs remained as Emily applied some Dior perfume to her skin.

'I love my mutts so much,' Emily said as she played with the two doggies who were happily wagging their tails.

She then walked downstairs, as her friend had texted that she would be outside any minute. Her mum and dad were watching TV in the living room.

'Olivia will be here in a minute,' Emily said.

'OK. Shall I order you two a takeaway?' asked her father, who was overweight and had a kind face.

'Yeah. Last time you cooked we had too much food for words. I said we would order from the noodle bar,' Emily said.

Emily's father gave her a twenty pound note for the takeaway.

Olivia rang the doorbell and entered Emily's house. Her two dogs greeted Olivia with friendly woofs and wagging tails. She followed Emily upstairs to her room after saying hello to Emily's parents.

'You look great,' said Olivia as she hugged Emily. Olivia had long, blonde hair and was a lot shorter than Emily. She was very pretty and had pale skin and blue eyes.

'Thanks. How's your week been?' Emily said.

'Just a bit stressful. Waiting to see if I passed my first year,' Olivia said. 'Doing a BTEC in fashion at college and studying a distance learning A-level in Italian isn't easy you know. My private tutor for the A-level is great if not a little dull.'

'I'm sure you've done great. I know I'm stressed as well,' Emily said.

'You'll be off to uni soon,' Olivia said. 'We should go to Italy and visit my parents' holiday home before you go. It's near Rome so we could go shopping and go to some of the good clubs.'

'That would be amazing.'

'We would have such a blast there. It would be the time of our lives,' Olivia said.

The two girls talked about how excited they were about the summer. Olivia suggested that they should book the holiday to Italy once they got their college results.

'I bet there will be loads of hot guys at the University of Avenna,' Olivia said.

'I hope so. It's not too far that I won't be able to see people on weekends and of course my dogs!'

'Oh God, tell me about it. I can't go a day without giving Fluffy a hug. I haven't thought about where I'm going to go to university after college. Maybe I'll take Fluffy with me.'

Emily ordered the girls' food from The Noodle bar, which was a restaurant they both liked to dine at that also did takeaway. Emily noticed how Olivia's bag was Chanel. Olivia had a lot of designer clothes due to her family being millionaires.

The two girls took a selfie together before the food arrived. They took photos on each of their phones. Emily loved taking photos of herself on her mobile. She would often upload them to Myspace.

The girls ate their food when it arrived and talked about boys. Olivia had a boyfriend who she had been dating for three months.

'Do you think you will find a boyfriend this year?' Olivia said.

'I don't know.'

'Maybe sometimes you are too fussy with guys,' Olivia said.

'I'm just looking for something particular,' Emily responded.

Olivia would be sleeping in the air bed tonight.

The two girls ate their noodles and watched *Buffy the Vampire Slayer* on the small TV Emily had in her room.

Emily wanted to talk to Olivia about something important. Recently she had experienced a weird mood swing and her parents were really worried. She had gone to the doctor who had given her a week's supply of medication. Yet the week's worth of medication had finished and she was starting to feel on edge again. She had a follow-up appointment next week, yet she was finding it hard to cope.

'Olivia?'

'Yeah?'

'I think I might have bipolar.'

Olivia frowned and looked at her seriously. 'Why do you think you have bipolar?'

Emily told Olivia what had been going on recently. How she had felt so strange. Her mum had explained to the doctor how Emily had always struggled with depression as well as these new feelings that she was experiencing.

'I don't know much about bipolar to be honest. Yet if you do have it, I will be there to support you,' Olivia said.

'Thanks,' Emily said. It meant a lot to her that Olivia was accepting of all that she had told her.

The next morning the girls enjoyed pastries that Emily's father brought to her room. They didn't talk about Emily's bipolar; instead they discussed how excited they were regarding getting their college results.

'Once we know that we've both passed, let's book that holiday to Italy,' Olivia said.

Emily agreed that it was a good idea, yet she was unsure if she wanted to go. Lately, she had been feeling unsteady. She knew that she and Olivia always would go out drinking when they went out together. Last summer they had gone to Download music festival together and drunk quite a lot of alcohol.

'I think that's a great idea,' Emily said. Yet she knew she was concerned about the trip. Her mind was too uneasy lately and she didn't want to bring Olivia down after she was making such an effort to include her in things.

Olivia's dad picked her up in his sleek sports car a half an hour later. Olivia hugged Emily as she left the house.

'See you soon,' Olivia said as she waved goodbye.

***

A week passed and Emily began to feel more weird. She started to find it hard to sleep. She stayed up at night listening to music and drawing in her sketchbook. Her drawings were brilliant but disturbed, pictures of people who looked so upset. The drawings were full of forlorn faces with tears in their eyes. She considered her art darkly themed and was proud of the creation she made in her sketchbook.

When Emily did sleep it was only for a few hours. She would wake up full of a hurried energy with ideas of how she would become a great painter. She had this idea that she must set up a website for artists all over the world and the site would make her a millionaire. But she didn't vocalise these ideas to anyone.

'I'm worried about you,' her mother said on the day that her BTEC results arrived in the post.

Emily hadn't been able to pick them up over the last few days because she had not been sleeping properly. Emily had been talking to herself a little and her parents didn't want her to go into college to pick up her results in the fear that she would embarrass herself in front of her peers.

As Emily opened her results, her mind felt consumed with bigger thoughts about how her art business idea would make her a great entrepreneur. She hastily opened the letter. She had got three distinctions in her BTEC, the highest pass a student could receive.

'Three distinctions,' Emily said.

'Well done, love. Those are top grades. I'm so proud of you,' her mother said in the darkly lit living room of their house.

'I think I might put a hold on university next September. I've got this idea and I was thinking of going on *Dragon's Den*. I've got the most amazing business plan.'

'Don't be silly, love,' sighed her mother. 'I think you need some rest. I don't think you and Olivia should go to Italy next week. You're not acting normal lately.'

'It will be fine!' Emily's voice was high pitched and her thoughts were running a mile a minute.

'Just put the holiday off for a couple of weeks. You've got till September till you start university at Avenna. Olivia's house in Italy isn't going anywhere.'

'OK. Fine. I'll call Olivia and let her know to put the plans off for a while.' Yet Emily was secretly thinking to herself how she would prove to her mum that she was fine. Yet when she was alone in her room, she forgot to even call Olivia to check on the flights.

Emily had seen on Olivia's Myspace how her friend hadn't done as well as she would have liked in college. Olivia had been very upset in her post about her college results.

Emily began to make a website about how she would sell art and pitch her business plan. She was sure that people like Alan Sugar from *Dragon's Den* would see it and think her idea was phenomenal. Yet the website was made from a free domain and was more a pitch concept than anything real.

Then she posted a comment on Olivia's Myspace, '*You may be pretty but with results like that, you're not the brightest spark are you.*'

Her friend responded quickly, '*What the heck has got into you lately? I don't know, but I love you anyway. I'm booking the holiday, so please don't be out of character tomorrow when we meet for our vacation! Xox.*'

'*That's fine, book the flights tomorrow, I can't wait to see you,*' replied Emily. Emily then signed off on the computer.

That night Emily stayed up all night working on her website. She also applied to be on the next series of *Dragon's Den*. She took an hour to fill out the application while listening to heavy rock music.

By the time Emily woke up the next afternoon, she had a furious voice message from Olivia who said she had wasted hundreds of pounds on the flights only to have Emily not show up at the airport. Olivia was in tears. She said she was so cross with Emily and that her father had said Emily was not good enough for her.

Emily's head spun. She had totally forgotten about the plan to rush off to Italy. She felt furious that Olivia's father had said she wasn't good enough for Olivia.

She began to laugh hysterically. She wasn't sure what time it was, it was like time itself had a new meaning. All she knew was that everyone would pay.

Her mum was out taking the dogs for a walk and her father was out at work. Emily went into the kitchen and emptied out the medicine box. She found a couple of packets of paracetamol. She took these tablets with water. Emily was not sure how many paracetamols she took but she knew she had taken an overdose.

After ten minutes she began to panic and the realisation and terror of what she had done kicked in. As she began to scream, her mother returned home with the dogs.

'Emily, what's wrong?'

Her mother looked frightened.

'I've taken an overdose,' she cried.

'Oh you stupid girl!' her mother screamed.

The dogs looked scared as they huddled together. Emily's mother called the ambulance.

'WHY?' shouted her mother.

'I don't know. I don't know what's wrong with me,' Emily said as tears ran down her face and the cold terror of her actions made her feel dizzy.

When the ambulance arrived, a man and a woman were preparing to take Emily to Stoke Mandeville Hospital. Emily's mother showed them the packet of empty paracetamol that her daughter had taken.

'Oh dear,' said the male paramedic. 'We'll take care of things from here.'

Emily's mother was told to stay at home while the paramedics drove Emily to hospital.

***

Emily had to undergo an unpleasant procedure to clean her blood, which involved a drip attached to her arm. She kept crying and vomiting. 'I don't want to die,' sobbed Emily.

'You won't die,' said a Spanish cleaner with kind eyes.

Emily blacked out and the next thing she knew it was the next day. A black woman with a concerned expression was standing next to her in the hospital.

'Emily Green?'

'Yes?'

'I'm Fiona, a mental health nurse at Brown-Tree Psychiatric Hospital. You've been put under a section two of the Mental Health Act, which means you will be kept in hospital for up to a month. This is happening because we think you have bipolar and the fact you took an overdose.'

Fiona said that everything would be OK. The mental health nurse explained to Emily how she had fully recovered from her overdose and it was lucky that she had not taken many paracetamols. The nurse frowned as she spoke. Emily wished that the deep sense of misery she was experiencing would evaporate.

'Let's go, Emily,' said Fiona as she escorted Emily out of the hospital.

They went into another ambulance on their way to Brown-Tree Psychiatric Hospital. Emily believed that she must be bipolar, why else would she have done something so reckless and for no good reason at all?

She thought about her parents and how worried they would be. It was late July. If she could get through this month at Brown-Tree maybe she could go to Avenna and study art in September. A wealth of anxious thoughts filled her mind as she travelled to the psychiatric ward.

The hospital was old-fashioned-looking and the building was tall and made of dark stone. Emily followed Fiona into the ward.

Emily's mum and dad were waiting at the reception. Her dad was shaking and her mother was crying. Emily felt too ashamed to hug them or even speak to them. Emily watched them look at her with a lost expression she had never seen in their faces.

'She's on a section two,' Fiona said to Emily's parents.

'How long will she be here for?' asked Emily's mum.

'A month,' Fiona said.

'Look after her,' pleaded Emily's mum.

'We will take good care of her. I will call you tomorrow,' Fiona said.

'I'm sorry,' Emily said to her parents, who looked back at her with such sadness in their expressions.

'We know,' said her mother.

Fiona the mental health nurse took Emily into the main body of the ward. Emily was frightened as she followed the nurse and heard the sounds of the hospital.

Chapter 5

Emily was given her own room in the Brown-Tree ward. She had felt so low as she slept in the room that just had stark furniture and none of her things. Her thoughts were consumed with guilt as she remembered taking those deadly tablets. The room was small with a bed and a washbasin and there was also shower cubicle. It looked bleak and void of the comfort that made her bedroom at home feel like a safe place.

She felt like a loser and couldn't comprehend how she had been so reckless. She didn't understand her motivation to try and end her own life. It was like a mad and wild energy had made her hysterical where she only saw into the black abyss of death. Yet she was alive and was grateful of this.

She had been given heavy medication which made her sleep deeply. It was two in the afternoon when she woke up.

Emily was nervous to venture into the ward. She didn't have her phone. Outside, she could hear shouting that sounded like someone was very upset. She was hesitant to exit her room and enter the main ward, yet she knew she couldn't stay locked up in this bedroom for the duration of her time here.

As Emily left her bedroom she looked around the ward. The walls were painted yellow. People old and young were walking around mumbling to themselves. The nurses were in blue scrubs and had calm expressions on their faces.

Emily nervously walked past a woman who was talking to herself. She didn't feel as crazed as she had the other day, yet she felt that must be due to the medication she had taken. She felt as though she was hungover and also had a heavy sluggish sensation in her limbs and one which made her mind feel like it was being slowed down.

A tall guy with curly blond hair approached her. He was wearing baggy jeans and a red hoodie.

'You're Emily, right?'

'Yes.'

'I heard all about you. Don't do that again. Suicide isn't a good way to die.'

'Does everyone know that I tried to kill myself?'

'People in this place talk, we're like a big family here. Welcome to the crazy house.'

He introduced himself as Clive. He explained he also had bipolar and this was his second time in Brown-Tree.

'I don't know what I was thinking,' Emily said. 'It was like some mad energy was controlling my actions.'

'That's bipolar for you. You'll get on the right meds and then you will start feeling more like your old self again,' he said.

Clive introduced Emily to the other patients. Some of them were Emily's age and others were older than her parents. There was even an elderly lady sitting in the corner of the TV room. One of the patients was badly burnt and her appearance was frightening. Her features were hard to make out and she was disfigured by the burns on her skin. Emily instantly felt sorry for the lady.

Emily was dreading the next month at the ward. Clive promised that he would keep an eye out for her, explaining to her that some of the patients were nice yet others were not to be trusted.

'You'll be all right. You're only in here for a month, I'm on a section three, which can last up to six blooming months,' Clive said.

'What are you going to do when you get out of here?'

'I'm moving to Liverpool. My sister lives there.'

Emily followed Clive around the ward. The old fashioned architecture with its stark brown walls and old windows that looked like the building had been put together in the 1950s made the place feel gloomy, as though it was a place for those that were forgotten by the world due to their afflictions. Emily could imagine sick people throughout the years wandering around this ward. She imagined their essence lingering in the walls and dark halls.

Emily and Clive were allowed to go into the communal gardens of the hospital. It was much prettier here. Whoever had done the gardening had put a lot of care into the flowers. There were potted plants scattered neatly in the garden and well-kept trees.

They sat together on a bench, observing some of the other patients who seemed to look happy enough, which Emily found surprising. Clive asked her about what she wanted to do when she got out of the ward. Emily told him how she was planning to go to university in September to study art. Yet as she described these things, she heard the strangest voice. It was loud and sounded as if it was coming from somewhere behind her. The voice exclaimed that she would never go to university and would be stuck here forever.

She didn't tell Clive what she was hearing. She did her best to seem normal; after all, if she wanted to get out of the ward in a month's time, she needed to reclaim normality. She smiled in the right places and didn't bring up any of the thoughts stemming to the surface of her mind, which she knew Clive would deem out of the ordinary.

***

The days that passed since Emily's admission to the ward were intense. The voice would constantly remark on everything that Emily did. She believed it was coming from somewhere in the ward as opposed to her own mind. The voice seemed as though it was outside or within the walls.

Brown-Tree was full of people shouting and acting abnormally. Emily felt frightened at times when people became aggressive in their body language and would have to be taken into padded cells when they acted too crazy or in some way violent towards the nurses. A loud siren would ring and the nurses would take them into a padded cell where they would be sedated with drugs.

The hospital wasn't all gloom. There was an art room which Emily attended every afternoon. The hospital staff said that Emily should go each weekday because she was a gifted artist. Emily knew she was talented in art due to doing so well at her college course. She believed fine art was her calling in life.

Emily enjoyed painting in this room with other patients. The occupational therapy leader was impressed when Emily told him she had a BTEC in art.

'You're very talented indeed,' said the occupational therapist, whose name was David.

Emily was sitting in the art room, which had only one other patient who seemed calm, yet his hands were shaking. Emily was painting on an A3 canvas using acrylic paints. She was working on a picture of her mother. The painting showed her mother from the waist up with her thick glasses and kindly face. It had a light-purple background which made the picture feel calm.

'Thanks. When this place is behind me I'll be studying fine art at the University of Avenna.'

'Oh, how lovely. Yes, I've heard of Avenna, it's in East London, isn't it?' asked David.

'That's right,' Emily said.

'I take it you will be moving to London for your studies?'

'That's the plan,' Emily replied.

Emily had been in Brown-Tree for a week. She felt half asleep from the medication she was given at times. Yet at other times her whole body felt jittery and like she was a Duracell bunny. She would talk non-stop about ideas of setting up an art website.

'I was going to start an art business website,' Emily said with an animated expression on her face.

'Do you know much about business?' David asked.

'I know I'll be successful, I can feel it.'

David sighed. 'I'd get your bachelor's degree first. Then you will have some real world experience.'

'I guess,' Emily said, knowing how she desperately wanted to become famous in the art business world and believed that she was destined for this.

'Well, get better first and you will do wonderful things,' David said.

***

Emily would talk to just about everyone on the ward. She felt so full of energy and ideas. As she wandered around the psychiatric ward she greeted the patients with wide eyes and expressed how she had the idea of the century.

'I'm going to make it out of this town, I'll be a millionaire when my social network for artists gets off the ground,' Emily said to a woman whose name she didn't know. The unwell lady looked at her with a bewildered expression.

As Emily walked around the ward she noticed the cleaner looked merry. She was completely sure that the cleaner named Jack was Alan Sugar in disguise. The cleaner had grey hair and, even though he was a man in his late fifties, he looked cared for. As Emily walked up to him he smiled with a calm expression.

'Are you in disguise?' Emily asked him.

'Disguise?' Jack looked surprised.

'I know you're Alan Sugar and that you're watching me so you can hire me for my art website when I get out of here. Will I have to appear on *Dragon's Den* first?'

Jack looked at her with a sad expression on his face. 'If I was Alan Sugar I wouldn't be working as a cleaner and living in a council house. Now, love, you just put those ideas out of your head and concentrate on getting better.'

'Well, I guess so,' Emily said.

'That's right, love. Now, you just enjoy this place the best you can, it's not all doom and gloom. You'll be back to normal life in no time,' Jack said as he walked away from her and continued to clean the ward.

Although she'd told him that she accepted what he said, Emily knew he was lying. What else could she do? Part of being in this place was acting and pretending that things were going to be OK. It was the only way she would ever leave the ward.

***

On the weekend, her mother came to visit her. She looked tired when she arrived. She was holding a Lidl bag, which she handed to Emily. The bag contained toiletries and sweets. Emily was glad to see her mother, she needed familiarity in this turbulent time of her life.

'I'm so worried about you,' said her mother. 'Your father's really depressed. He's gone into one of his downward spirals after what you did. I think when you get out of this place, you should take a year off before starting at Avenna. You need to heal from whatever it is that caused you to have this episode.'

'I need to go to university in September,' Emily pleaded. It meant everything to her to become normal again.

'I really would prefer if you wait till the following September. You'll be a year older and wiser. I'd be worried sick about you moving away from home so soon after all of this.'

She said she would think about what her mother said, but she knew she just wanted to be a normal girl and move to London. She wanted her friends to see her as successful and healthy.

Her mum promised that she would visit again on Wednesday next week. *I'm so glad to see my mother and feel devastated to hear dad's in one of his depressive cycles,* thought Emily. Emily knew it was because of what she had done that her dad was deeply depressed. It was understandable, she thought to herself. She struggled to get on with her dad at times. She found his depression exasperating. When her dad was depressed, his presence felt like a black energy in the house that drained Emily. If Emily would talk about positive things, her dad was always dismissive and negative when he was in one of his cycles of low-mood. She would often vent to her friends about how exasperating it was.

***

Clive was always shouting at the nurses. Emily was saddened that on her second week at the Brown-Tree ward, Clive was taken upstairs into the more secure ward, for patients that displayed violent behaviour.

Emily texted Clive each day to see if he was OK. She had learnt a lot about him over the two weeks since they'd met. He had studied anthropology at The University of East London. He was very intelligent and kind. Emily hoped that she would be friends with him after she left the hospital in two weeks' time.

Emily lay in her room with the window open, which was letting a fresh breeze in the room. Someone knocked on the door, and Emily called for them to enter. A mental health nurse entered. Her name was Willow and she had short, black hair and thick glasses.

'I just wanted to have a chat with you,' Willow said.

'OK,' Emily replied.

'The doctors on your ward round have agreed you need to stay here for another month. So it will be six weeks before you can go home, that is if you can get better. The doctors have handed you a letter which explains that we feel you have bipolar-affective disorder.'

Emily scanned the letter, feeling frightened at the diagnosis.

'What does the affective bit mean?'

'It means your illness is a combination of bipolar and schizophrenia. You've been expressing not only mania but delusional behaviour. I know this sounds scary, but you will get better and get to live a normal life with medication.'

Emily began to cry. It would be too late to go to Avenna in September if she was here for another month. How would she ever get back to normality?

'Why don't you come into the TV room? I'll sit with you for half an hour.'

In the TV room, Willow talked to her about how she would be entitled to receive disability living allowance benefits. She explained how they weren't means-tested, so even when she worked she could receive this money.

'Money's always welcomed,' Emily said.

'I'll book the benefits officer to come and see you next week, does that sound good?' Willow said with warmth in her voice.

Emily thought that Willow was kind. She hated knowing she had an official diagnosis of having a mental illness, yet was glad she would receive benefits that would help her manage financially. Thoughts spun in Emily's mind as the voice from afar screamed that she was doomed never to study at the University of Avenna.

***

The benefits officer was a kindly man with a wrinkled face. He filled out the disability living allowance forms for Emily and explained she would most likely get the middle rate, which was three-hundred and fifty pounds a month.

As the benefit officer talked about other benefits she may be entitled to in the future, Emily heard the voice that seemed to come from nearby scream, 'You'll never get out of Brown-Tree and go to the University of Avenna.'

'That will be great,' Emily said. Emily felt sad because she was unsure if she would ever make it to Avenna. This illness seemed like it would last forever.

Emily had been thinking about Olivia a lot lately. She was currently in Rome with her family at their holiday home. The two girls had arranged to meet up when Emily was out of the hospital. Yet her friend sounded cold on the phone when they had called each other. It was evident to Emily that Olivia didn't regard her the same way, now that she was officially someone with a mental illness.

Emily remembered Olivia's remark. 'You'll be on Benefits Street.'

David asked Emily how she was finding the ward. Emily said it was OK, but boring at times. On one occasion, Emily had to go out into town with a nurse. One of her friends had seen her there and the nurse was wearing a visible Brown-Tree name tag. Her friends had gazed at her with a superior look in their eyes. Emily knew that her friends were judging her because she was gaining weight. She also knew how people were gossiping about her overtly on social media. She knew this because when she did go home, she saw comments on her Myspace wall when she checked her laptop. This made Emily feel awful. She felt as though she was losing control of all normality in her life.

***

During the ward round, a panel of doctors, psychiatrists and mental health nurses would discuss Emily's treatment with her.

'I think I must be getting better,' Emily said, feeling jittery. 'Yet why are you all pretending that Alan Sugar isn't monitoring me in the ward? I know that man isn't a real cleaner.'

The doctors in the panel all made notes on their laptops and looked up at her.

'Emily, would you step out of the ward-round for five minutes while we discuss things?' said Dr Ora.

Emily walked out and made herself a cup of tea in the communal kitchen of the hospital. It was still morning, so the kitchen was clean. In the evening, tea bags would be everywhere and all the orange juice cartons gone from the fridge.

Emily returned five minutes later to see her mother looking solemn. She made eye contact with her mother, yet she looked away.

'We feel it would be best for your quetiapine to be upped a little,' said Dr Ora. 'We feel this will help with your delusional beliefs.'

Emily's mum was at the ward round and agreed with the doctors that this was for the best. Emily had been at the ward for a month now. She had four more weeks to go before she would have a chance of leaving the hospital.

'Will Emily get help from anyone in your team when she leaves this ward?' asked her mother.

'We think she should have a care worker assigned to her, they'll support her in her ambitions to go on to university. If she does choose to study in London like she planned, we can transfer her to the London borough of Newham where Avenna is located when she's ready to start her studies,' said the doctor.

Afterwards, Emily was allowed to go home for three hours with her mother. Her mother offered to get her some new clothes from River Island, which was one of Emily's favourite shops.

'I'll order you some bits online,' her mother said as they walked to Emily's family home. 'You're a size twelve now, aren't you?' Her mother looked nervous mentioning how Emily had gained two dress sizes.

'Yeah. I'm no longer a size eight,' sighed Emily. 'I'd really appreciate it.'

It was nice being home. She talked with her dad. She said she was sorry for her reckless actions a month ago. He told her that when he had divorced his first wife, he had done something similar due to depression.

Emily talked with her dad for a long time. She said some crazy things, expressing her delusions, yet her father simply nodded.

After talking with her parents, her dad made dinner. Her mother kept watch over her as she went into her bedroom. Misty and Muttly followed her upstairs, they were so excited to see her.

'Will you pack up all my clothes for me?' Emily said sadly. 'There's nothing bigger than an eight or ten in my whole wardrobe. I'm getting benefits anyway, so I can buy a whole new set of clothes.'

'When you get out of here, you can join the gym across the road. I'll give your clothes to the RSPCA charity shop for now. Hey, when you go to Avenna, I'm sure you'll be slimmer, and have reason to revamp your wardrobe once more,' said her mother.

After a dinner of spaghetti and garlic bread, her mother walked Emily back to the ward.

'I just want to be normal again,' Emily said. Emily's mother stood in the doorway of her room as Emily sat on the bed.

'You will, love, I promise you, you'll find normal again. I love you and everything's going to be OK.'

***

During the final two weeks of her stay at Brown-Tree, Emily began to get better. The doctors explained how she was on a dose of medication which was almost correct to allow her to be stable with her condition.

She no longer heard the shouting voice or believed that Jack was Alan Sugar. She didn't feel dizzy with energy and talked a lot less to the nurses and patients at the ward.

During her final two weeks, she spent a lot of time hanging out with Clive in the garden area. They had deep conversations about the meaning of life.

'This life is a journey of learning,' Clive said. 'You have to learn to be a good person and make a difference to the world in a positive way. That's how you pass or fail in this life.'

Emily handed Clive a gift of an oil painting she had done of him in the art room of the hospital. It was done in a realistic style and it really captured Clive's Germanic looks.

'You are an amazing artist,' Clive said as he looked at the painting and smiled.

'I'm glad you like my artwork,' Emily said, feeling happy in this moment.

***

By the time Emily was ready to leave, she had a lot of gifts from patients in the ward. A lady with schizophrenia, who kept calling the police from the communal phone in the ward, had given her a jewellery box. Another girl had given her a bottle of Britney Spears perfume.

As Emily packed up her things and prepared to leave the ward, she felt excited for the future. She didn't feel beautiful like the girl she had been when she was slim. She was self-conscious of her new body and disappointed that none of her friends had visited her. Yet that was also a relief.

Once she had packed up her things, the room looked almost as if it had already forgotten her. She wondered what the new patient would be like who inhabited the room once the cleaners had purged it of her presence.

As she left the room, Willow accompanied her to the main reception where her mum was waiting to pick her up.

'Keep well, Emily, let's hope we don't see you in here again,' Willow said.

'I hope so too,' Emily said, wishing she could give Willow a hug but knowing it wasn't appropriate. So instead she simply smiled.

Emily signed out at reception and walked with her mum down the street toward their house. They didn't live far from Brown-Tree. It was a hot day in August and that evening it was beautiful.

Chapter 6

Emily was glad to be home. The first night back, her parents made a fuss over her. Her dad made the most extravagant homemade pizza with the freshest mozzarella.

That night, Emily checked in on her personal PC in her room and saw how people were referring to Olivia's 'crazy' friend. She knew that these acquaintances were referring to her. It made her feel heart-sick and insecure, thinking of people that had once wanted to be like Emily and were now looking down on her. They saw her as an unstable and crazy girl.

That night she took comfort in the company of her dogs, Muttly and Misty. She was glad of the presence of the Collie-type mongrel and small West-Highland terrier. She remembered how she had been twelve when they got Muttly from Battersea Dog's Home, she had been so excited about getting a dog. Then when she was fifteen, they got Misty from a local breeder. Both dogs were beautiful additions to the family that made the house feel like a true home.

Emily kept in touch with Clive, who was still at the Brown-Tree ward. He was getting a lot better, and Emily planned to go for a meal and the cinema with him when he was able to leave the ward. She would text him once or twice a day; he had become a new best friend in her life. Someone who understood what it was like to be on medication and have a life-changing mental illness.

***

Emily had to attend day hospital on weekdays. It ran from nine in the morning till three in the afternoon. There were a few other people Emily's age. She met a young guy who must have been a couple of years younger than she was; he told her how he had developed an anxiety condition and that was why he was here.

The day hospital was a five-minute walk from the Brown-Tree hospital. It was located in a small house that had been converted into an informal hospital. The mental health nurses at the day hospital seemed more relaxed than the ones at Brown-Tree, who had to deal with people who were much more sick.

Emily no longer believed her delusions. Nor did she experience the mania that had left her talking a mile a minute and extremely restless. She was on a medication called quetiapine that left her feeling extremely tired. Her mum had to help her wake up each morning for the hospital sessions.

It was nice being around other people. Emily added a girl at the day hospital to Facebook who had dyed blue hair and was a year younger than she was. The girl expressed how she wanted to do the access course, because she had failed her A-levels due to a breakdown.

Emily was feeling a lot happier in herself. She knew she was getting better. She felt a sense of hope in the air. Even though her body was bigger now, she wore a size twelve in all her clothing items. She hadn't uploaded new photographs of her body on Facebook. Myspace was going out of fashion and Emily had deleted her account because she was embarrassed by the manic things she had blogged about when she was ill.

She had rambled on about her art business that she believed would make her a millionaire. Her 'friends' had been cruel to her, stating she needed to see a psychiatrist and that she was going insane. It hurt because it was pretty much true; Emily had been ill.

As Emily sat in the white room of the day hospital, with a large flatscreen TV above her with the news on quietly, she remembered just how sick she had been only a few weeks ago. The art business had no logic to it, it just seemed like strange energy to her now. Emily had no mind for business and wondered why she had been delusional about these things.

The psychiatrist, whose name was Dr Pharrell, was a middle-aged black man who had a very serious manner; he was pleased that Emily was taking the time to practise self-care.

'Next September you will be ready to start your studies at Avenna,' he had said with a serious expression written on his face. 'Art school will wait a few more months.'

Emily was a little sad that she wouldn't be starting university in September. She wished she could magic herself fully recovered. Yet she also knew that she was somewhat traumatised by her illness and needed some time to recover. The University of Avenna had been very understanding about her deferring her place for a year; her mother had sorted all that out via emails with them.

It was a warm day in August, the weather was full of damp heat. Emily was wearing a white summer dress and had her long black hair straightened. During her illness she had washed it way too much and with cheap shampoo, and she had damaged its condition considerably. Yet when she straightened it and put some serum on the black strands, it looked pleasant enough.

'I can't wait to get out of here,' said the girl with blue hair, whose name was Alexa.

'I know the feeling,' Emily said.

'You're an artist, aren't you? I saw the work you did the other day,' Alexa said, referring to the paintings Emily had produced in the group art class they had as part of occupational therapy.

'Yeah. Not this September but next September, I'm studying a degree in art.'

'Wow. I can't draw for shit,' Alexa said. 'I want to study economics at university. I was doing it at A-level at the Floyd but then I got sick. I'm going to do the access course next September, my mum wants me to get better first.'

Emily talked with Alexa, who was nice. She was glad to make a friend in day hospital, but could tell, apart from being both alternative, there was something missing from their interactions. It was a chemistry that friends require.

That afternoon when Emily walked home from day hospital, she thought how in a year she would be at Avenna. Her life would be changing and hopefully she would manage to keep well. She hoped that she would find romance at Avenna. The thought scared her a little, as intimacy had always been attached to her beauty. She didn't feel as beautiful anymore now that she was a little bigger. People had assured her that she still looked gorgeous, yet she found it hard to believe them.

***

By the time it was October and summer was over, Emily was discharged from day hospital. Her dad had stopped working ten years ago due to depression, yet he was doing OK these days. Emily's mum was working as a pharmacist in the local Boots.

Some days Emily's father would drive her to the big Tesco near Stoke Mandeville, an area which melted into Aylesbury. He would buy ingredients for lovely meals that they would cook during the week. Her father had been a chef for a fancy restaurant in London, and he was an extremely talented cook.

Emily had joined the gym near the house. She hoped she could get slimmer by the time she started Avenna. Sometimes Emily would feel self-conscious in Aylesbury. She felt as though people laughed at her and would make little comments that were cutting. She didn't really discuss with her parents how she deeply wanted to get away from the town. She knew it would only upset them, because the house wasn't in a good enough condition to sell and move somewhere else. Her mum and dad had worked hard to provide Emily with a good home, and she knew it would only hurt them both if she said she was starting to hate this town.

On Saturday afternoons Emily volunteered in Scope, which was a charity for disabled people. She had never worked in a charity shop before and really enjoyed the experience. There was a young guy in his mid-twenties who had autism and an eastern European young woman who worked with her on a Saturday. Emily liked serving at the till and sorting through all the stuff that people donated. Everything in the shop was sold for one pound at present, because the shop had such a huge influx of donations.

Emily was receiving DLA, which was three hundred and fifty pounds a month. She also received ESA, which was four hundred and eighty pounds a month. It was a lot of money for her to have and more than she had got when she worked in a local supermarket before she had become ill.

Emily would give her parents two hundred pounds a month which they used to pay some of the household bills. Yet she still had a lot of money to herself which she used to get new clothes and save some money for next September at Avenna.

She was fairly happy. She felt a little lonely and had felt incredibly self-conscious one evening when she and Clive had gone to the pub. She was sure she had heard people whose faces she recognised remarking on her, yet maybe it was just her insecurity.

Clive was well now, which was lovely to see. His medication made his hands shake and he was soon moving to live with his sister in Liverpool. She would miss Clive; he had asked her to visit him, which she thought would be a really good idea. It would be lovely to see Liverpool, as it was somewhere she had never been.

Olivia wasn't the same. She had expressed that things were back to normal yet her once best friend was more distant. Emily saw her friend was hanging out with new people at Aylesbury College whose pictures Emily didn't recognise. Olivia still looked perfect in Emily's eyes. Her slender blonde friend was the picture of a successful teenager.

***

It was November when Emily and Olivia finally went out together. They had met for a coffee a few weeks ago and Emily had felt awkward. Olivia had been her best friend since she was seventeen, yet now things felt strained. Olivia looked uncomfortable in Costa, she was looking around and frowned when she saw Emily.

Yet Olivia had expressed how they needed one of their nights out. She said she didn't mind that Emily wasn't able to drink much anymore.

After going to Costa, that evening they went back to Emily's house. Emily was very aware things weren't the same. There was less enthusiasm in Olivia's description of college or her personal life. When they dressed for the local club, Emily felt fat but she didn't say anything.

'You can have one drink,' Olivia said as they queued for the club.

'Sure,' Emily said. She was wearing a black pencil dress. She would never have had to wear tummy Spanx before to make her stomach appear flat, yet now she did. Yet the body-shaping underwear hid Emily's slightly bloated stomach and accentuated her hourglass figure.

Emily wore flat, black shoes which showed off the recent tattoos on her feet. She had flowers on each foot which looked delicate and beautiful.

Olivia didn't have any tattoos, and her hair was blonder than it had been last year. It was a white colour and looked in pristine condition. She held a Gucci bag and wore a red tube dress and high heels.

When they got into the club they danced for a while. Olivia had about three drinks and Emily had two. Emily was happy to be around her best friend again and having a good time. They drank alcopops as they danced to the loud music of the local club.

Emily knew she shouldn't really have had any alcohol yet she wanted to fit in. The club was full of young people dancing and drinking.

Emily watched as a tall and handsome guy approached Olivia and asked to dance with her. Olivia talked with the guy for a while. While Olivia was talking with the guy, Emily looked at her phone and thought how she doubted anyone would ask her to dance. She didn't feel like the Emily of the past who got a lot of attention from guys.

'He was cute, did you give him your number?' Emily asked when Olivia returned from walking with the handsome guy.

'No, he was from Wales. It's so far away, I don't want a boyfriend on the other side of the country,' Olivia said. 'Let's get some more drinks. Oh shit. Let's get some soft drinks, I remember you can't drink as much now.'

As they went to the bar, a young guy offered to buy Emily a drink. He commented on how she was one of the better looking girls in the club, yet she found it hard to believe him. She also wasn't attracted to him.

'You could have let him buy us our drinks! Oh well!' laughed Olivia.

When the bar closed, the two girls got a taxi to Emily's house. Emily noticed how Olivia was texting in the taxi and had mumbled her reply to a text. 'No, she's not crazy anymore,' she had sighed.

It hurt Emily to think that Olivia obviously thought she had been crazy. She had said she had looked up bipolar and schizophrenia, yet Emily knew in her heart things weren't the same.

Olivia had seemed a little uncomfortable all night and had been looking around far too much. It was evident that her best friend was no longer that. She had become a shadow of a best friend.

As they watched True Blood on DVD on Emily's new Xbox 360, she thought to herself how the friendship was a shadow of what it had been. Emily hadn't really told Olivia about Clive or what the other young people with illnesses whom she had met had been like. Olivia no longer talked about college with her. She knew how Olivia was going to her holiday home in Rome with her friend Stacey from college. Emily guessed that Stacey was Olivia's new best friend. Olivia had stated how they would be drinking a lot and the holiday wouldn't have been suitable for Emily. She understood and accepted that their relationship had changed. Yet it did hurt.

That night was the last time Emily went out with Olivia until the summer before university, when she went to a movie and drinks with Olivia and her new boyfriend. He seemed really nice and was very good-looking. Emily was happy for Olivia, feeling as though he was a good match for her.

Summer seemed to slip away. The year that had just passed had consisted of seeing so many films with Clive at the local Odeon and working as a volunteer in Scope. Emily had gained more weight and her medication made her so tired at times. She was now a size fourteen to sixteen, yet she knew she couldn't stall Avenna for another year.

As she packed her things in preparation to move to the East London university, she thought of all the memories of her life in Aylesbury. From childhood to her teenage years. She was twenty years old now. She was a great artist and she felt if she worked hard she could get a first in her bachelor's degree.

She would have to improve her confidence, because she knew she had to learn to accept herself in this fat body. Yet the prospect felt hard.

'You're growing up and starting your career as a wonderful artist,' said her mother as she packed her clothes into the suitcase. They were getting the train to Avenna tomorrow.

'Things will be good at Avenna, I can feel it. They have to be,' Emily said as she smiled at her mother, who looked back at her with a happy and hopeful expression.

Chapter 7

Emily was excited about her second year at Avenna. Kordell had met with her the previous night and compelled her so that she wouldn't accidently affect any of her classmates' destinies. Yet he had warned her that his compulsion wasn't strong enough to stop her powers forever. She would have to learn how to harness them.

Emily liked Kordell, he was kind and soft natured. She had spent the previous night learning so much about his life. How he had been twenty-five when he was turned. He admitted to her how his maker named George had forced him to kill an innocent human.

Kordell recounted how the experience had haunted him all of his immortal life. Emily felt that any vampire who was heartbroken by killing just one person couldn't be that bad. Kordell had explained to her what most vampires are like, how they kill with no remorse.

Kordell explained how when vampires kill a person, that human is erased from time. The whole world forgets they existed, even that person's parents. The world adjusts to their absence. Kordell explained it was due to a witch's spell in the medieval times.

Emily would have been terrified to join the supernatural world, yet Kordell had compelled her to feel calm. His soft, almond-shaped eyes had willed her to feel at ease with this change in her life.

Emily was relieved Parker hadn't contacted her again. It was now September and Emily was enrolling in her semester A modules at the University of Avenna. She was excited to travel to university with Shakira and Lisa, who both were also enthusiastic about their degrees.

***

On the first Monday when Emily had classes once more, Shakira travelled with her via train to Avenna, as she also had a Monday morning class. Shakira was wearing short shorts with thick tights, with a red top and green blazer on.

'This year is going to be the best, we can have parties at the house,' Shakira said.

'That will be good,' Emily said, thinking how she wanted to shy away from parties.

'We need to find you a nice young guy, someone who doesn't play mind games with you the way Parker-the-arsehole did.'

'He was OK, I just wasn't right for him I guess.'

'Yeah, well he could have figured that out sooner. Anyway it's not like you two slept together, so I guess... it's all learning experience.'

'What classes have you got this semester?' Emily said, wanting to forget about Parker and not lament on dating in general.

'Ugh, clinical psychology this morning.'

'That's nice. I've got abstract art this morning.'

'Wow. I wish I could swap degrees with you. Not that I'm any good at art. Yet I regret taking psychology as my subject.'

'Have you thought about cashing in your credits if you're unhappy and maybe studying something else?'

'Nah. I'm already here in the second year. Two more years of this shit and I can get a well-paid job, get a mortgage on a house and find a handsome fellow.'

'That sounds like a good plan,' Emily said.

The girls talked about life in general. Shakira said she was happy at the posh pub in Holborn that she worked in. She described how some of the preppy guys that came in the bar were so handsome and how one of them had asked for her number.

'So, yeah. Maybe I'll have a preppy boyfriend by the end of the week,' smirked Shakira.

'If he's nice. It might be good. Rich and handsome is a good combination,' Emily said.

Emily was a little concerned about Shakira. She smoked strong weed in the evenings and Lisa had expressed concern that she thought Shakira had started using class A drugs. Lisa had said she found the remnants of cocaine in the bathroom.

Emily thought Shakira looked put together in the way she dressed. Yet she was changing through her supernatural curse. She could sense that Shakira felt unstable in herself.

When they arrived at the metallic grey building which was the campus for the University of Avenna, Shakira hugged Emily as they departed and made their way to class.

Emily was excited to see her classmates. She had most of them on Facebook and knew who was returning for the second year and who had dropped out or failed the first year. Most of the students were returning.

The art class was fairly small. Her group were group A and there were four other groups of students taking different versions of the fine art bachelor's degree. She would meet with the other students occasionally, yet the twenty-odd students who made up group A were the people who made up her experience of studying art.

Aron was the first person she saw when she arrived in class. He was tall and broad with blond hair and blue eyes. She knew he had a crush on her last year, yet she hadn't felt the same. He was actually quite wealthy yet something about his personality was off; even though there were other aspects of his character she liked as a friend.

'I knew I'd see you again,' Aron said. 'Miss has all the talent. So, how was your summer?'

'It was OK,' Emily lied, thinking how it had been the most frightening summer of her life. She had learnt about the supernatural world. A world Aron would never know about.

Emily talked with Aron, who told her how he had gone to France for his holidays. He bragged about sleeping with a good-looking French girl and Emily cringed.

When the other students arrived in the art workshop, Emily was glad to see the professor. She was a woman in her sixties with dark brown hair and dressed in a hippy tie-dye T-shirt and brown flares.

The first morning class consisted of talking about the second year and how the abstract art module would work. Emily was glad when they got to the point of discussing what projects they would work on. Emily wanted to look at contemporary non-famous artists, as she had focused on classic artists throughout her first year. She wanted to be inspired by a painter on the internet she had found and work on creating a similar piece of abstract art for her first assignment, which, along with her essay, would make up ten percent of the module's grade. The professor thought her ideas were great.

'I always look forward to your projects,' said Professor Jane Calendar.

After the lesson Emily met up with Shakira for lunch. She noticed how Shakira seemed to be buzzing with energy.

'Are you OK? You seem different than you were earlier?' Emily said, worrying that she may have influenced Shakira with her powers.

'I'm fine. I'm just high.'

'What did you take?' Emily said.

'Coke,' mouthed Shakira.

Emily felt worried to have it confirmed that Shakira was doing cocaine. It was disconcerting to know that someone she now considered a best friend in her life was taking such a serious drug.

'Maybe you should go home for the day, it's not a good idea to do stuff like that at uni.'

Shakira made a remark Emily didn't hear. 'I'm fine. I haven't got any more classes today. Thanks for your concern, mum.'

Shakira talked a mile a minute for ten minutes. She seemed full of confidence and more aware than usual of her beauty. She had such long, sleek, black hair and she kept touching it and making eye contact with guys around her.

Emily was glad when it was time for her to go to her next lesson, which was art skills, a module they had in each year of the degree. The module consisted of practising art skills and writing essays on technique and practise as an artist.

Emily watched Shakira make her way out of the university café. She knew she was going home and hoped that her friend wouldn't get high at uni again.

Emily enjoyed the rest of her day in her class. She enjoyed small talk with other students. She was happy to see familiar faces in her class. She had a few close friends in the course, yet most people she regarded as acquaintances.

****

Emily was as happy as she could be, considering she had become a Destiny Walker. She felt as though a heavy brick was upon her back, emotionally weighing her down. Yet she was also content with a lot of her life, such as how university was going and her living situation in Lewisham.

Emily was worried about Shakira. She remembered teenagers at college when she had lived in Aylesbury, who had dropped out of the art BTEC due to their drug use. She recalled how there had been two students in her art class who had been affected by drug use. She didn't know what to think of Shakira's habit. She was scared to offer her friend advice in fear that it might fracture the relationship.

On Saturday night, after Emily had finished writing a short essay for university earlier that evening, she waited for Kordell to visit with her. She left the window open and waited for the house to become quiet; his voice was so soft that no one noticed when he visited.

At two in the morning, Kordell slipped in through the window. His blond hair looked freshly bleached and his afro curls looked well kept. He was wearing a black T-shirt and jeans.

'Good to see you, Emily.'

'Likewise.' She was genuinely glad to see her vampire friend. In the last few weeks she had begun to trust him.

'I come with some interesting news. I found another Destiny Walker through a connection of mine. His name is Rodger and he lives in America. Yet I have spoken to him on the phone, and he's agreed to come to England to meet you.'

Emily was excited at the prospect of meeting another person who had the same curse as she did.

'When will he be able to visit England?'

'I wanted to check you were happy to meet with him first. He's a strange guy, I have to admit that. You might be a bit freaked out when you meet him. He's a prime example of how the curse can ruin a person's life.'

'Oh.'

'I am going to help Rodger as well as help you.' Kordell's eyes lit up. 'I have a friend, her name is Agnes and she's a very powerful witch. When she is next in town, I plan to introduce both you and this Rodger guy to her, I think she'll be able to help the both of you.'

'Can she take away this curse?'

'No. Only by giving the curse to someone else can you rid yourself of being a Destiny Walker. You have to make the decision whether you want to do that, or if you are going to learn to manage your powers and how you control your will and intention around others,' Kordell said.

Emily couldn't bring herself to give the curse to someone else, not yet. She imagined what that woman with the silver wig who violently knocked into her must have been thinking when she decided she would pass her curse on to Emily. Perhaps she didn't know what she was doing.

'How are you anyhow?' Emily asked.

'I'm so so,' sighed Kordell. 'This life, living as a vampire isn't for me. I tolerate my existence.'

Emily didn't know what to say, she didn't want to pry into what being a vampire was like. She knew that Kordell didn't feed on human blood like most vampires. She also knew the terrifying truth that humans who were killed by vampires were erased from the memories of everyone who ever knew them. Yet Kordell had compelled her not to fear him and something deep inside her soul told her she could trust him. Something that knew he was one of the good guys.

He had gone into detail on how not all vampires were evil. Vampires had souls and they could either live a virtuous immortal life or let the bloodlust turn them into sick creatures of the night.

Emily talked about how university was going. She told Kordell about her art projects. He expressed interest and asked questions about what inspired her to paint.

'From the work I've seen of yours, you are certainly gifted,' he said.

By the time it was three in the morning, Kordell expressed that it was time for home. He needed to stay away from the early-morning dusk; although it would not kill him, the rising sun did burn his skin.

Emily knew how vampires couldn't walk around in daylight and how he would die in direct bright sunlight.

'Until next time, take care Emily. I'll text you soon and let you know when Rodger is coming to England.'

'Thank you so much for all the help you've given me, I'll see you soon,' Emily said.

Kordell exited her room. Emily knew she would take a few hours to wind down after seeing him. Spending time with her vampire friend always heightened her senses. She needed a fair few hours for exhaustion to creep into her before she would be able to sleep.

Emily took a fresh canvas onto her easel and begun to paint. She worked on a self-portrait in acrylics which was very distinct to her style. She wasn't able to finish the painting, as the paints took time to dry, yet Emily needed to create art – it gave her a purpose in this world.

She then worked on some sketches of figures in her sketchbook that she kept for her own personal enjoyment as opposed to university work.

By the time it was seven in the morning and the sunlight was soaking through her curtains, Emily was tucked into bed. She was so tired, and the anxiety of spending time with Kordell had somewhat worn off. Tomorrow was a new day. Kordell would help her, she had to believe that she would learn to harness her powers.

Chapter 8

Emily spent a great deal of her time painting in her room. She would listen to a varied array of music while she worked on art pieces. She had to create a lot of artwork for her degree and she loved it with her whole heart.

It was almost October and the weather had become much more spiteful. The air was crisp. Emily would wear a heavy green coat when she went out. She wore thick tights underneath her rockabilly dresses.

Lisa knocked on her door while she was working on sketches. Emily asked her friend to enter. Lisa was dressed in a gothic black dress and her long green hair had been curled.

'Hey,' Lisa said.

'How's things?'

'Good. Well sort of,' sighed Lisa.

'What's up?'

Lisa fidgeted with the sleeves of her gothic lacy dress, 'Aiden found a graphic design competition for creating book covers for self-published authors. The prize for the winner is a two-hundred-pound Amazon voucher. He thinks I should enter but I'm scared I'm not good enough.'

'You'd be great at that,' Emily replied, feeling that it would be a wonderful experience for Lisa.

'It's just I've still got so much to learn about graphic design. I'd actually like to design book covers, it just feels like a lot of pressure. I don't want to get disheartened about my degree studies if I do miserably in the competition.'

'I think sometimes you have to put yourself out there. Just let the results of the competition wash over you, just say to yourself that you won't let it get you down if you don't win.'

Lisa was beautiful with a small face and slender features; she was tall and elegant. Emily was very fond of her friend who she had met in her first year of university in halls of residence.

'I guess you're right,' Lisa said. 'I'm a great graphic designer. I've got this,' she beamed.

Emily was pleased that her friend felt positive. The two girls discussed how their courses were going. Lisa talked about Aiden and how he had a job interview at a local music shop.

***

Emily went to the cinema with Shakira during the week. The two girls invited Lisa, but she was too busy with the graphic design competition. Emily and Shakira saw the latest Spiderman movie at Greenwich cinema and went for a Mexican meal.

When they got back to the house it was eleven at night, and Lisa was still working on her book cover for the graphic design competition. Lisa's hair was unbrushed and she looked as though she had not slept.

'Lisa, are you OK?' Shakira said.

'I'm fine,' sighed Lisa, 'just busy.'

Emily felt a tense energy in the air. It made her feel a sense of shock as she wondered if her friend was under her influence. Had she somehow accidently affected Lisa?

'You look tired,' Emily said to Lisa.

'I said I'm fucking fine, now go to bed and leave me alone!' Lisa shouted.

Emily was shocked and watched as Lisa closed her laptop and stood up.

'I'm sorry, I'm just tired. I'm going to bed. I hope the film was good,' Lisa said as she quietly walked upstairs.

'She's tense. Maybe she's been drinking too much coffee,' Shakira said.

'Perhaps.'

When Emily had spent a few minutes drinking tea in the living room with Shakira, she then went upstairs so that she could be alone. In her room she texted Kordell and explained that her housemate seemed to be behaving weirdly.

'*I don't know if I've influenced her,*' texted Emily.

Kordell texted back stating that she was to arrange for him to come to the house, stating how they were classmates and he would know if Lisa was under her influence.

***

The next day Kordell arrived at the house on Grace Road. He rang the doorbell and Emily greeted him.

'Good to see you,' she said.

Kordell followed her into the living room. Shakira was at work, yet Aiden was at home, as was Lisa.

'Hi,' said Aiden.

'Hi. I'm Kordell.'

'Interesting name,' sighed Aiden. 'So how do you know the delightful Emily?' There was a sarcastic tone in his voice.

'We're both studying art together,' Kordell quickly replied.

'So, you're an artist too,' Aiden said. 'Well, that's great. I'm going upstairs but do introduce yourself to Lisa, that's my girlfriend. I'm sure she'll be happy to meet one of Emily's cool friends,' Aiden said, and then exited the living room and stomped upstairs.

Kordell stood with a confidence that only handsome people possess. He said hi to Lisa, who had just walked into the living room and was holding her laptop.

'You're Emily's friend, we saw you at the Fox and Ferkin a while back.'

'Yeah, that's me.'

'I'm really busy or else I'd love to chat,' Lisa said. Her eyes looked red, as though she hadn't slept that night.

Yet Emily watched as Kordell worked his compulsion over Lisa. He looked into her eyes and pulled Lisa into his gaze. Emily watched as Lisa seemed to sway and look lost in Kordell's eyes.

When Kordell released Lisa from the compulsion, the young woman looked confused.

'God, I'm fucking tired. I'm going to have a coffee and then go upstairs. I've got to finish my design tonight.'

Emily and Kordell watched as Lisa hurriedly made her black coffee with three sugars. She took it upstairs, carefully holding her laptop under her arm.

When Emily and Kordell were alone in the living room, she whispered to him, asking if Lisa was under her influence. The vampire nodded and looked upset.

'I'm afraid so. Just do what you did last time, imagine the influence you have over Lisa as though it's a physical thing, like a rope or a belt, and then let it break. If you concentrate hard enough, this should work.'

Emily imagined the rope like Kordell had described when she had influenced Parker. She imagined a golden rope tied around Lisa, wrapping around her beautiful gothic outfit and her slender arms. As she pictured the rope, she imagined how they were infused with dark magic. She imagined a scissor which had good magic radiating from it, magic to undo the evil she'd accidently leaked onto Lisa. As she cut the imaginary rope in her mind and envisioned it falling to the floor where it evaporated into dark energy, she heard Lisa swear upstairs.

'What's the matter now?' shouted Aiden loudly.

Lisa and Aiden could be heard arguing upstairs. Kordell whispered to Emily that he would stay until late, to ensure that Lisa was no longer under Emily's influence.

A half hour passed and Lisa stopped arguing with her boyfriend. Emily and Kordell were sitting on the black sofa in the living room, watching Mock the Week on the chunky, large TV.

Lisa ran downstairs, dressed in her pink pyjamas which accentuated her slender frame. Her make-up was washed off, yet she hadn't properly got rid of all the eyeliner and it was evident she had been crying by the way the liquid eyeliner had run down her face.

'Are you OK, Lisa?' Emily said.

'I can't enter that stupid competition. I don't know why I believed I could. What's a two-hundred-pound Amazon voucher to me anyway? I'm a rich girl, aren't I?' Lisa was shaking. 'I'm going to sit down with you guys for a bit and have something to eat, I just want to forget about the stupid competition.'

Lisa made herself a cheese sandwich and drank a can of Diet Coke. She sat on the other sofa in the living room.

She asked Kordell what sort of art he liked. He expressed how he was inspired by artists from the 1950s, saying that the time was one that took him back to an era in fashion he had always liked.

'Yeah, me and Emily love those 1950s style dresses. A lot of gothic shops make dresses in that style but with bats or skulls on the print.'

'You're both very elegant young ladies,' Kordell said.

'You should come out with us. You live locally, right, as you go to the Fox and Ferkin. We could go there some night, maybe next week,' said Lisa.

'Perhaps. I'm pretty disorganised with my studies, so I'm a bit bogged down at the moment, but I will do my best to meet up with you both again,' said Kordell.

When Lisa went back upstairs, she said goodnight to Emily and Kordell. When she was gone, the vampire confirmed that Emily's influence had worn off and that her friend would be fine.

'What am I going to do? I didn't even know I'd influenced her.'

'I'm going to introduce you to Rodger and get some more advice from my witch friend, Agnes. She's researching Destiny Walkers, as it's a rare supernatural occurrence.'

'I'm scared to meet Rodger. I'm freaked out to see what he will be like, you said he's been a Destiny Walker for ten years.'

Kordell looked sad as he looked at Emily. 'You're a good soul, I want to be able to save you from your curse. It's very important to me and I also want to help this Rodger when he arrives in London. I'll let you know as soon as he books the flights from America.'

'I can't imagine what I would have done if I had never met you. How on Earth would I have managed this curse without you, never knowing it was something supernatural?'

'Well, I'm here and I'm never leaving you,' Kordell said.

Kordell stayed with Emily for another hour. He asked her about university. He asked her about how her family were doing.

Emily told Kordell how her parents were happy. They had nearly paid off the mortgage of their three bedroom house. She described the terraced cottage to Kordell, saying the house was a bit tatty but nice.

Kordell told her about his mother, who was a great pianist, and how they had been rather wealthy. She had played in opera halls around Europe. Kordell had grown up in London. He had been studying a master's degree in sociology when he had been turned into a vampire.

Kordell described his maker, whose name was George. His vampire maker was eternally in the body of a young man in his late teens. George had blond hair, and Kordell described his appearance as verging on ugly. Kordell expressed how he hated becoming a vampire, he felt it doomed his soul to darkness.

Emily knew the story of how he had only ever killed one human during his immortal life as a vampire. How it had been due to being under the influence of his maker, George. Kordell was still a good person in Emily's opinion. She did not feel he was a murderer, because he had been acting like a puppet under a compulsion he couldn't control.

'I'll call you soon,' Kordell said as he put on his smart, black, wool coat and prepared to leave the house.

'I'll see you soon. Thanks for everything.'

'You are most welcome,' Kordell said, and then he left the house.

Emily got a can of Diet Coke out of the fridge. She looked at her phone, seeing it was almost two in the morning. Shakira would be back from her job at the pub in an hour.

When Shakira returned home, she openly took cocaine in front of Emily. Emily would have loved to influence Shakira to stop taking drugs, yet she knew it would have terrible consequences. So she instead decided to not think on anything regarding an opinion for her friend's drug use.

Shakira and Emily talked about university. Shakira complained about her course and said that after her bachelor's degree she was done with education.

'I'm hoping to study a master's in fine art,' Emily said.

'No thanks for a master's degree for me,' laughed Shakira. 'Yet I think that would be really good for you. You're a bloody fantastic artist.'

The girls talked a little about their plans after Avenna. They all wanted to continue renting the house on Grace Road for their final year.

'I'm going to travel after Avenna,' Shakira said. 'I'm thinking of visiting Peru. I've got some friends I've known for years online who live there. Everything's so much cheaper in South America.'

'I feel kind of scared at the prospect of travelling,' Emily said, feeling embarrassed to admit that truth.

'We should all go on some amazing holiday when we're done with uni. I can't risk it this summer, I'll probably have re-sits like I did last year. My third class degree awaits me. Meh, maybe I'll get a two-two.'

'Any degree is better than no degree,' Emily said, hoping her words would be encouraging.

'Yeah, my parents said they're proud of me. No one in my family's been to university. First generation right here. Not everyone's mum has a master's degree,' Shakira said as she grinned in a friendly manner.

The two girls talked until the early hours of the morning when they retired to bed. Emily hoped that Lisa would feel better tomorrow.

***

Lisa seemed back to her bossy yet kind self in no time at all. She was ordering Shakira and Emily to walk faster when they went to Sainsbury's. She complained that the house wasn't tidy enough and made everyone spend their days off tidying.

After the tidying session, all four of the housemates were sitting on the sofas eating Domino's pizza and drinking soda.

Lisa looked at her iPhone and looked very puzzled. 'How can this be?'

'What's up, Lisa?' Shakira said.

'I've got an email from the graphic design competition saying I won it, that I won the first prize of the Amazon vouchers and for my cover to be used by a successful indie author for their new book.'

Aiden smiled. 'I knew you'd win, that's why I submitted your entry after you gave up.'

Lisa was obviously shocked, yet a broad smile broke across her face. She got up and kissed her boyfriend on the cheek.

'Oh, I love you so much at times, more than I can say,' Lisa said to Aiden.

'I knew you'd win. I just wish you hadn't got so crazy stressed. It's all over now. Do you think you'll buy a copy of the book with your cover?'

'Yeah. I think I will. I'll also buy some nice perfume and DVDs with the voucher,' Lisa said, smiling from ear to ear.

Emily ate her pizza in silence. She was happy for Lisa regarding her achievement. Emily knew that Lisa was a great graphic designer and that this book cover would be a great credit on her CV as an artist.

Chapter 9

Emily was wearing a pretty, 1950s-style, black dress today at university. She had recently got her hair cut at a salon and it was looking in better condition. Her dyed-black hair was straightened.

As Emily entered the university library, she walked to the vending machine. There was a tall, chubby guy wearing a long, blue cardigan in front of the machine; he turned to her and smiled with soft, grey eyes.

'Shit weather today,' said the guy.

'Yeah,' agreed Emily.

'I'm Dean.'

'I'm Emily. What are you studying?'

'I'm a first year counselling student,' Dean said.

Emily observed how he had an attractive face. 'Oh cool. I'm in my second year of an art degree.'

'Oh, that's cool. I'm not arty myself. More of a reflective person.'

'How are you finding the University of Avenna so far?' Emily said.

'I like it here. I'm only from around the corner in Beckton. I didn't want to get into heaps of debt so that's why I applied here.'

'It's awful that the government are planning to raise tuition fees to nine grand a year next year,' Emily said.

'Too right it's bloody awful. They know it's going to put poorer students off university. I hate the Tories.'

Emily couldn't help but smile. She noticed how Dean had a loud speaking voice.

'Do you have Facebook? It's always nice to make friends with other students studying different things here,' Emily said.

Dean got his phone out at once. 'Sure. What's your full name? I'll add you now.'

'I'm Emily Green.'

Dean Adams added her to Facebook. He talked to her for a few more minutes about his degree. He said he was enjoying it and told her how he had studied counselling up to level three at the local college in Newham.

When Dean got his can of Pepsi and left the library, Emily felt glad that she had potentially made a new friend. He seemed really nice.

***

When Emily got home at six in the evening, Shakira was smoking weed in the living room. Shakira was wearing a short, black dress that showed off her long, tanned legs.

'Hey,' Emily said.

'Hey.' Shakira's voice was mellow. 'Oh my gosh, you're the first person I'm going to tell this news. Please don't freak out.'

'What is it?'

'Well... thing is, you know I wasn't enjoying my studies at Avenna. Psychology was OK when I was a teenager doing A-levels, but at university it's just been a headfuck. So, anyway, I dropped out of my degree.'

Emily felt sad to hear this. She knew Shakira was from a family that had really been proud that she had got into Avenna, as it was quite a hard institution to get in to.

'You have to do what's best for you,' Emily said.

'I know, right. I was thinking, so next year I'm going to stay living with you guys here. As you know, I love living with the lot of you, even if Aiden is a stuck-up twit. But then next year, I'm going to see if I can work in Peru or another South American country. I want to see the world, you know. I want a year of living abroad, then I'll come back to London. I was thinking of studying social work instead.'

'That would be amazing,' Emily said.

'I don't want to study it at Avenna. I mean I'm glad I went there and I'm glad I met you guys, but I like the idea of studying at a different London uni when I try studying again. So my plan is I save up as much money as I can this and next year, then I work abroad and really see the world. When I come back to London, I was thinking of applying to study social work at whichever London university will take me. Also I'll have a certificate of higher education in psychology as well as my A-levels and shit.'

'That sounds like a really great plan,' Emily said. Emily felt it was good for Shakira to look into studying social work if it was indeed something she was more interested in than psychology. She hoped her friend would be safe in South America.

'I think I'd make a great social worker. I don't really ever talk about this, but I was picked on a lot in high school. It made me a stronger person in some ways, yet it's haunted me in other respects.'

Emily expressed how she was sorry to hear that her friend had been bullied in high school. Shakira told her how the University of Avenna were sending her certificate of higher education in the post. The two girls agreed that Shakira should do something to celebrate when she got the certificate, as it was a great achievement in itself.

The two girls ordered pizza from Papa Johns while they watched *Friends* on TV and talked about their plans.

***

Over the weekend Emily enjoyed watching *Buffy the Vampire Slayer* on iTunes. She drunk Diet Coke and sat in her room, which was a little too messy to be healthy. A lot of her clothes were on the floor and dirty dishes sat next to her laptop.

Emily texted with Kordell over the weekend. He was arranging for her to meet with Rodger, who was another Destiny Walker. He was also in contact with a powerful witch named Agnes, who had said she would help both Emily and this guy Rodger.

Emily felt hopeful for the future. It was almost half term for semester A of her second year. She was looking forward to Halloween. On the weekend of half term she was going out with the household to the Fox and Ferkin; yet in the week, she was going home to Aylesbury.

She deeply looked forward to seeing Muttly and Misty, her most beloved dogs. She spoke with her mum on the phone a lot, yet her dad wasn't much of a phone person.

Emily had been talking a little with Dean on Facebook. He had messaged her on Saturday evening after liking two of her photographs the previous day. She saw from his profile how he had three cats at home and loved video games.

Emily enjoyed talking with Dean. He was intelligent and friendly. When he asked her if she'd like to go to the cinema to see *Black Swan*, she wondered if he was asking her out on a date.

Emily agreed that she would meet up with Dean next weekend. She hoped it was a date, because he seemed nice. Yet as she imagined dating Dean, feelings of insecurity screamed in her subconscious.

***

On Sunday evening Emily went with Shakira to the pub where she worked. It was Shakira's day off, yet her friend wanted to show her workplace. Her manager had agreed to change her hours from part time to full time.

Shakira was wearing a green jumpsuit and small heels. As the girls sat in the posh pub in Holborn, Emily thought how beautiful her friend was. Shakira had glossy black hair, dark eyes and an oval face. Not only was her friend very good-looking, she was also kind. Emily had become very close friends with her since moving to the house in August.

Emily and Shakira sat in the pub. It was six in the evening and it was fairly quiet. There were some rich-looking, middle-aged men having a quiet pint at the other end of the bar.

Shakira ordered both of them a glass of red wine. Emily sat on the soft, red, leather sofa and looked around at the pub which had beautiful artwork that she recognised as being from the Victorian era. Emily thought to herself that she was glad good things were happening in all their lives. She was careful not to wish any new events for any of her friends, afraid she would curse them with her will.

Emily looked in the direction of the bar and saw that Shakira was waiting for the barman to finish serving two guys. They were dressed in gothic attire and Emily smiled to herself, thinking how they both looked attractive from what she could see of them.

Emily then turned her attention to her phone. Olivia had texted her asking how university was going. Emily felt glad to hear from her old best friend. She missed her, yet didn't feel like things were the same now.

Olivia lived in an exclusive one-bedroom flat in Camden and was studying fashion at South Bank University. Her parents had bought the flat for Olivia outright when she started university last year.

Emily texted back, saying that she was happy with her studies and things were great living in Lewisham. She thought of how she didn't feel she could relate to Olivia and her easy life anymore.

When Shakira returned with the red wine, she was standing next to the two guys from the bar. One of them had fair Caucasian skin and long brown hair. The other guy, who was standing closer to Shakira, was of Hispanic appearance with short black hair, and had two lip piercings on his left side.

'This is Rafael and this is Mark,' Shakira said. 'They were just telling me how they study at the University of East London.'

'Wow. That's really near Avenna,' Emily said.

The two guys sat down at the table with Shakira and Emily. Mark, who was the English guy and had a rose tattoo on his neck, sat next to Emily.

Shakira told the two guys how she had just dropped out of Avenna and her plans to study in London after she travelled for a year.

'You need to do what inspires you,' said Rafael to Shakira. His hair was straight and he had a small amount of facial hair on his handsome face. His arms were covered in sleeve tattoos and he was wearing a Misfits T-shirt.

Rafael made a lot of conversation. He was obviously attracted to Shakira, as he kept looking at her. Yet he seemed nice and made an effort to ask Emily questions too. There was chemistry in the air between them; even Emily noticed this.

'I'm studying music. Mark's in my class. We both play in a shitty band.'

'What's your band called?' Shakira said.

'Jin-jack,' Rafael said. 'We're kind of a punk band. We're OK but you know, the music industry is a hard one to get into. We have a few pub gigs and it's fun.'

Shakira asked Rafael about the band. He told her how he was in the final year of a music bachelor's degree. He was twenty-four.

Emily enjoyed the wine and found the conversation interesting. When Rafael asked for Shakira's phone number, Emily was happy for her friend.

'Here's my number,' Shakira said.

'You're really beautiful by the way,' Rafael said, blushing ever so slightly.

'Thanks,' replied Shakira, smiling at the compliment.

Rafael and Mark left the bar, saying they were getting the bus back to their house in East Ham.

'Oh my Gosh,' Shakira said with an excited tone, 'that guy was so fit. I hope he calls me.'

Emily and Shakira had another red wine and talked for another hour in the pub. It was a little more packed by the time they left. Emily enjoyed the night air. They got the night bus back to their house in Lewisham.

Chapter 10

Emily was happy for Shakira, who had described her first date with the gorgeous Rafael. When Shakira and Emily had met him in the bar, he seemed so nice. Emily hoped that he would be a serious boyfriend for her Shakira.

Emily considered Shakira and Lisa both her best friends, people who she could trust. Although she couldn't tell them how she was a Destiny Walker and knew a vampire, she was able to let them into all other aspects of her emotional life.

Emily had her own date to be excited about. She was meeting with Dean in the afternoon. They had arranged to go to the cinema in Greenwich. Emily was meeting Dean outside the cinema at six in the evening.

Emily thought about how it was a date. She had been talking with Dean each day on Facebook messenger and had his phone number. She liked him a lot, he was smart and interesting. There seemed to be a warmth to him which radiated even from his messages on Facebook.

When Emily arrived at the cinema, she was wearing a pink polka dot dress, and she wore a plastic flower in her black hair, which was straightened.

'You look nice,' Dean said as he greeted her.

Emily asked Dean how university had been this week. He said he was enjoying the assignments and described his classmates. He told her how many of the other students were a lot older than him.

Black Swan was an excellent movie. It was tense and theatrical. When the two exited the movie, Dean looked at her with a sweet expression in his grey eyes.

'The movie was good; shall we go to the restaurant?' he said.

They left the cinema and entered the Mexican restaurant in Greenwich that she had recommended to Dean. She had been there a few times with her housemates.

'How are you finding your art degree?' Dean said as he smiled at her.

'I love it so much. Avenna is such a great place to study.'

'I chose it because it was so local to me. I have to say I'm really enjoying the course so far.'

Emily asked Dean what he wanted to do after his bachelor's degree at Avenna. He described how he wanted to practise as a youth counsellor for teenagers. He told her how when he was in his teens he had experienced a fair amount of depression and that was why he wanted to help young people.

'You'd make an excellent counsellor.'

Dean thanked Emily. They ordered fajitas and chips. The meal was delicious, and Emily was really loving Dean's company.

'Have you had many girlfriends?' Emily asked.

'Only one. She lived in Swansea. We were together for a year, but as you can guess it was long distance and we would only see each other every few months.'

'I've never had a long distance relationship. I've not really had a serious boyfriend. Just sort of gone on the odd date here and there.'

'I was eighteen when I had that girlfriend in Swansea. I haven't had a girlfriend since. I really think you're nice, Emily, so let's just enjoy the evening.'

They ordered a decadent ice cream sundae after their dinner. Dean told her about his video game collection and how he loved his Xbox 360 and PS3.

When the date was over, Dean got the train back to Beckton and Emily took her train in the opposite direction to Lewisham. Dean expressed how he wanted to see her again.

'I'd like to see you again too,' Emily said, and then kissed him on the cheek.

Dean blushed as he waved goodbye and made his way to his platform. Emily thought how lucky she was to have met someone so sweet and nice. She hoped that the next date would be just as lovely as this evening had been.

***

The next day Emily was to attend a supernatural pub with Kordell. He met her at the train station at nine in the evening and they travelled to Mayfair. They made very little small talk during the journey. Emily noticed how his jacket had the Vivienne Westwood crest on it. She wondered if Kordell wore a lot of designer clothes.

When they arrived at Mayfair and walked to the pub, which was inside one of the exclusive flats in this part of London, Kordell seemed to relax.

'It's just going to be you, me and Agnes tonight. Yet she throws extreme parties, or so I've heard... they're not really my scene.'

'What are they meant to be like?' Emily asked.

'Alcohol flowing like it's water. Agnes likes to use her magic to create optical illusions to impress her friends.'

Kordell had told Emily about Agnes. How he'd known her for a long time and trusted her. He explained how Agnes was a good witch and wanted to help Emily. He also warned her that she had a cutting way of addressing people and could often seem rude.

When they arrived at the flat, Kordell rang the doorbell. After a few moments Agnes answered. She was wearing a Chinese print, red dress and was tall and very slim. She had short brown hair and a sharp, beautiful face.

'Kordell, always good to see you.' Her tone was flat. 'And this is Emily, I've heard so much about you.' Agnes ushered to them to follow her into the flat.

The property was decorated like a bar, with black walls and posters of bands on the wall. Its regal architecture made it seem beautiful and somewhat a shame to be decorated the way it was, in Emily's opinion.

Inside the main living room there were red velvet chairs. Little tables hosted wine bottles readily awaiting future guests.

'Kordell, you must come to one of my parties, you know being undead doesn't have to equate to being dreadfully boring.'

'Maybe one of these days,' Kordell said. 'Emily's powers are growing. What are your plans to help her?'

Agnes surveyed Emily, narrowing her eyes. 'Her power is immense. She's dangerous, Kordell... Yet I can understand why you want to help her. She's an innocent and didn't deserve to be dragged into the supernatural world.'

'She needs to learn to harness this power or else consider transferring it onto someone else,' said Kordell.

'Quite right. Well, give me a while and I'll speak with my elders about what magic can soften the influence of a Destiny Walker. Rare thing to become.'

'We're meeting with a young man from America who obtained the same curse,' Kordell said. 'I think it would be beneficial for you to help him too. He sounded quite unwell when I spoke to him.'

'Fine. Witch and charity case it is for me then,' laughed Agnes. 'Very well. I'll help Emily and this other Destiny Walker. Just promise me, darling, if I help them, you'll party with me when they're able to look after themselves.'

'Very well,' Kordell said.

'Fabulous.' Agnes clapped her hands and walked to where there was champaign on ice. 'A toast, to friendship.'

Agnes poured them all a glass of champagne. Kordell looked annoyed. Emily drank the champagne, which was one of the most delicious alcoholic beverages she had ever drunk. It tasted very expensive.

Agnes reminisced about how she had known Kordell for many years. She expressed that in the thirty years she had known him, he had never gone to one of her parties. She also commended his good character and told Emily how most vampires were murderous.

After an hour in her company, Kordell and Emily departed back to Lewisham. Emily could feel Kordell's energy relax and was aware that he was remembering the time he had been turned. It frightened Emily to know that her powers were indeed growing. She didn't say anything to Kordell, as she saw the image of the blond vampire in his mind, the one who had turned him. The vampire had been named George and Kordell hated him more than anyone else in this world.

As they travelled by train back home, Emily could feel that Kordell was haunted by his past. She knew his dark secret, how his maker George had forced him to kill an innocent guy. A man who Kordell had feelings for. Emily was grateful that Kordell had told her this about him and would never purposely pry into his mind.

Emily thought how glad she would be when her powers were more under control. Life was never going to be normal, yet she had Kordell to guide her through this supernatural life. Perhaps she would find friendship with Agnes as well.

Chapter 11

Emily was glad it was half term. She had enjoyed a Halloween celebration with her flatmates. Shakira had brought Rafael, who was calm and friendly to everyone. Emily was really pleased Shakira had found a nice boyfriend. She was also happy with the start of her relationship with Dean, they were to go on their second date next week.

She spent the week in Aylesbury with her parents and dogs. She was so happy to have her two pets greet her with woofs and wagging tales.

Her father cooked a homemade Chinese meal that night. It felt good to be back in her spacious room in the three-bedroom house in Aylesbury. The pink walls and pictures of models reminded her of her youth and the person she had once been. Emily thought to herself that in the summer she would redecorate the room, making its focus more on art and the girl she was destined to be. The girl that was far away from the slender teenager she had been prior to becoming sick with schizo-affective disorder.

She had a stash of medication in her bedroom which she kept in the first draw just below her old TV with its VHS slot. She had an original Xbox in her room and it made her think of Dean and how much he loved video games.

After the delicious meal of egg fried rice, pork balls and noodles, the family sat down on the brown sofas and talked about things. Her dad no longer worked part time as a handyman and received disability benefits for his post-traumatic stress disorder. Her mum was doing well as a pharmacist and still worked at the local Boots.

Misty and Muttly sat next to Emily on the large brown sofa. Her mother was sitting on the desk next to the new computer she had recently purchased. Her dad was sitting on the armchair opposite Emily.

'I'm proud of how well you're doing at university,' her dad said.

'Yeah, the course is amazing. I'm on top of all my assignments so I can just enjoy this week off.'

Her dad talked about politics and what was going on in the news. It was evident that her parents were glad to have her back for the week. She could see they were pleased to see she was doing well.

Emily felt sad thinking how she could never tell them how she had become a Destiny Walker. Kordell had checked himself into a local hotel in the town, to keep an eye on Emily for her family visit.

Emily was so thankful to have the vampire in her life. He was a sense of safety amongst the chaos of what she had become. She truly trusted him and no longer felt the slightest bit of anxiety about what he was. She knew that Kordell hated being a vampire.

On her way to her bedroom, Misty and Muttly followed her upstairs. The little white West Highland Terrier and scruffy Collie mongrel meant so much to her. She would often ask her mum how the dogs were when she phoned her.

It was so good to spend time with them and give them cuddles and affection. Muttly said woof as she wagged her tail. The little West Highland Terrier seemed to salsa dance in the way she excitedly moved her body.

***

The next day she attended a beautiful green area with her parents and the dogs. Her dad brought the video camera and they filmed the dogs having a wonderful time.

Emily wore a green coat and comfortable boots. It was late October and the weather was fairly cold. Emily loved watching the dogs playing. It amused her to observe how Misty would run up to little dogs to greet them, while Muttly, who was the Collie, would ignore these dogs and simply go about her own business.

After the lovely walk the family returned home. Emily had always loved dogs. She remembered how when she had been a toddler the family had a Labrador cross, and she felt that her love of dogs was instilled by this gentle Labrador dog that they'd had as a pet at the time.

Emily made arrangements to meet with Olivia tonight. It felt nerve wrecking, because she no longer felt she could relate to Olivia. Olivia was a rich girl who had kept her model figure. She had a posh boyfriend and wore designer watches.

Emily remembered how they truly had been best friends before she had become sick. Yet that illness had been like a crowbar, yanking the fabric of friendship between them.

When Emily met Olivia outside Pizza Express, she wore a flowery rockabilly dress and black cardigan. Olivia was wearing a designer style suit that accentuated her tall and slender frame. She had an expensive-looking watch on. Her old friend looked at her with a half smile. Olivia's long platinum-blonde hair looked glossy.

'It's been so long,' said Olivia.

'I know. We've been meaning to meet for ages,' Emily replied.

'I noticed a guy called Dean on your Facebook, is that your boyfriend?'

'I've just started seeing him recently,' Emily said.

'Well tell me everything about him when we get in the restaurant,' Olivia said.

The two girls entered Pizza Express. Emily noticed how the waiter's eyes were fixed on Olivia. The waiter was tall and attractive. Once they'd ordered their pizzas and food, they begun talking and catching up.

Emily told Olivia all about Dean. There seemed an air of disinterest in Olivia, as though she didn't feel the friendship anymore. Emily could feel this radiating off her aura.

'I hope things work out with you and Dean,' Olivia said.

Olivia told Emily a little about her fashion degree. She said she hoped to get a 2:1. She didn't say much about her life in central London.

Emily had been hoping to invite Olivia to the house in Lewisham in the summer, yet she realised that her friend might only accept the invitation to be polite.

There were awkward moments of silence, followed by Olivia looking at her phone. When the meal was over, Olivia didn't even bother to take a photo of the two of them like she always had done when they were younger.

'I'll call you at some point, have a good rest of half term,' Olivia said.

'Sure, you too,' Emily said.

As Olivia got into her black sports car and drove back to Marlow, Emily felt her old best friend was now a stranger. She hadn't felt any of the old energy of the friendship.

As Emily walked home to her house in Aylesbury, she remembered the times she and Olivia had been inseparable as teenagers.

***

A day passed and Emily thought about her friendship with Olivia. She hadn't enjoyed her company that evening, she had felt her friend no longer saw her as the same person she had once been. Her powers made this clear to her.

She had new friends; Lisa and Shakira were her two best friends. She also had a budding romance brewing with Dean, who would message her every day online.

As Emily logged into Facebook, she saw Olivia had posted pictures of her friends in Marlow. She thought of how Olivia was at a restaurant in these pictures, yet she hadn't bothered to take a photo with her and Emily. She knew Olivia didn't want to be rude yet also didn't feel the caring magic she had once experienced being Emily's best friend.

Emily decided to unfriend Olivia on Facebook. She didn't think that her old friend would add her back or contact her again. She thought she would feel exceedingly sad at doing this, yet she realised it was part of life.

That evening Emily watched TV in her room in her family home in Aylesbury. She felt a sense of peace and was excited about enjoying the rest of her week. She was to meet with Kordell at the hotel he was staying at tomorrow.

***

Emily visited Kordell's hotel in a part of Aylesbury called Watermead. The hotel was quite luxurious, and he had booked one of the nicest rooms. The vampire greeted her, smelling of expensive cologne.

'How has your week with your parents been?'

'It's been good. I really enjoyed seeing my family dogs and parents. I felt kind of sad as I realised one of my old friendships was expired. You know that girl Olivia I told you about?'

'I remember you telling me about her.'

'I realised the friendship had expired. It did hurt me to make that realisation.'

'I'm sorry to hear that. Well, on a more positive note, I can sense from you how over the last week your powers have not been used. I am confident to say your family are safe from the curse.'

Emily expressed how thankful she was of this. She talked with Kordell about how she was excited to go back to Lewisham and work on her studies.

Emily and Kordell spent a few hours together. They watched a movie on the flat screen in his hotel. Kordell ordered her a taxi when it was evening time.

***

When Emily returned to Grace Road in Lewisham after her week away at her family home, she was excited to finish the semester at university.

She was looking forward to spending more time with Dean and truly getting to know him.

Chapter 12

Emily and Kordell waited in the airport for Rodger. Kordell said how he believed he would bring understanding to what Emily was going to experience from her curse.

When Rodger greeted them, he had a vacant look in his brown eyes. His hair was curly and he smelt sour. Rodger handed Kordell his suitcase to take.

'It's good to finally meet you,' Kordell said.

Rodger nodded and looked at Emily. 'I can feel the curse on you,' he said to her.

'How long have you had the curse?' Emily asked.

'Ten years,' Rodger replied.

They took Rodger to the fancy Hilton Hotel suite which Kordell had paid for. Rodger didn't seem to notice the opulence as he sat on the bed and seemed to stare into space.

'We're going to help you,' Kordell said.

'I believe that you think you can,' Rodger said. 'You know, this curse is a nightmare. I was on track to go to Vanderbilt University. Then one day I bump into this woman who looks like she's on crack, I think nothing of it. Then as the months pass everything turns upside down...' Rodger looked as though he was about to cry. 'I had this cat. His name was Chalkie. Anyway, one day I was so stressed I accidentally willed Chalkie to talk to me. The cat wouldn't stop talking and telling me how much he loved me yet hated the neighbour's dog. My mum was coming home soon and I couldn't un-will him to just meow like a normal cat.'

'What happened to the cat?' Kordell said.

'I had to kill Chalkie. I couldn't stop him talking and there's no way I could explain to my mum why the cat was fucking talking.'

'I'm so sorry that your curse has caused you such pain in your life,' Kordell said.

Emily felt terrified imagining what Rodger had been through. She truly hoped that Agnes would be able to help him. She needed to believe that there was hope for the both of them.

Kordell told Rodger he would be in the next room in the hotel if the young man needed anything. Emily could feel that Rodger was void of almost every shred of hope. He was hanging on by a string. Emily could feel how this was his final act of hope in changing the nightmare that had been his life as a Destiny Walker.

Emily left Kordell and Rodger, who would have to wait till tomorrow to see Agnes. She deeply hoped the witch would be able to help him. She didn't know the extent of Agnes's powers.

That night when Emily got home, she felt sad. It was a tragedy to see Rodger. She had only had her powers for a few months and dreaded to think of how they might manifest as time went by. Already she could feel things about people that normal humans would never know. She was trying so hard not to alter anyone's will. She had been happy that she hadn't influenced her parents when she visited them. Yet she feared that one day she might affect them, and the thought terrified her.

***

The next evening when Emily had finished a painting for university, she thought of how Kordell was soon to call her and let her know how things were going with Agnes and Rodger.

She hoped that Rodger could be saved; she had found him frightening, and the prospect of becoming similar terrified her.

'Any news on Rodger?' Emily said as she answered the phone to Kordell.

'Agnes is trying to teach him to will upon himself to bind his powers, something she will be working on with you too.'

'I hope it works.' Emily thought how lovely it would be to see Rodger have happiness again. It broke her heart to meet another Destiny Walker who was broken by the curse.

'I feel hopeful that Rodger will learn to bind his powers with Agnes's help,' said Kordell.

Kordell said he would call her in a few days and let her know how Rodger was doing.

When Emily finished the call with him, she thought about how in a few days she was going on her fourth date with Dean. The last two dates had been so romantic and innocent. She enjoyed the way he smelt so fresh. He would briefly kiss her on the lips and embrace her in the most warmest of hugs.

***

On their fourth date, Emily met Dean in Costa in Camden. He was reading on his Kindle when she entered the café; he looked up at her and smiled brightly.

'Hey you,' he said.

Emily and Dean left the coffee shop as he had already been waiting for her for half an hour. They looked around the market stalls in Camden. There were a lot of alternative fashion shops. As they entered one in the market that was a fancy boutique called Collectif, Dean offered to buy Emily a blue polka dot fifties-style dress.

'Are you sure?' Emily said, as the dress was sixty pounds.

'It will look beautiful, you could wear it on our next date.'

'You're so sweet, thank you,' Emily said.

When she tried the dress on in the fitting rooms, it indeed did look beautiful. She wasn't ashamed to pick up a size sixteen like she might have been with other guys. Dean was a fair bit larger than her, she imagined he must have been at least eighty pounds heavier than her. Yet all she saw was a beautiful man who she was really into.

After buying the dress, Emily and Dean got Mexican food at one of the food stalls. The burritos were delicious. They talked about university; Dean was doing really well in his course and felt it was possible he might get a first.

After the meal Emily and her boyfriend made their way to Camden's art centre, where they were to watch a live streaming of an opera. The opera was called Don Giovanni and the students had got the tickets free.

It was lovely watching the streaming of the classical music with Dean. She felt so close to him and could feel the goodness radiate from him.

When the opera was over, they travelled back home. When Emily was back in Lewisham, Dean texted her saying how he hoped she would officially be his girlfriend. She instantly replied how she would love that to be so.

Dean was good for her. He made her feel beautiful and at peace. She sometimes found herself daydreaming about how the romance would flourish over time. She didn't feel scared at the prospect of intimacy with him, she wanted to experience it.

Chapter 13

It was a Sunday afternoon when Agnes arrived unannounced to the house in Lewisham. It was pouring with rain and the witch was drenched. She was wearing a short, flowing, blue dress that clung to her slender legs.

Shakira answered, yet Emily was in the kitchen.

'Hi, can I help you?' Shakira said, not knowing who Agnes was.

'I must speak to Emily at once,' said the rain-drenched Agnes.

Emily walked to the door, seeing all this happening. 'It's fine, Shakira, she's my friend. Come upstairs, Agnes.'

When Agnes was in her room and the door was closed, the beautiful witch looked seriously at Emily; her makeup was smeared down her face and she was obviously freezing.

'I will need a bath and a change of clothes,' she said.

'Of course. Why did you visit anyway?'

'I did everything I could to teach Rodger to bind his powers. Unlike you, we found him years too late. He was so disturbed. I found him rather frightening to be alone with, yet I tried desperately to help him... I failed. When I went downstairs to make him breakfast this morning, he hung himself. When I got back with the full English breakfast, he was dead.'

'Oh no,' Emily said, feeling herself begin to shake with the revelation.

'He was too far gone. I did everything I could.' Agnes voice was low and she looked at Emily with a humanity in her eyes that Emily had never seen in the witch's expression before.

Emily put the hot water on and asked Shakira if Agnes could borrow some of her clothes. Shakira said she could keep a brown pair of tracksuits and a jumper.

'Why did she look so upset?' Shakira said as she handed Emily the clothes.

'Oh. She's failing her degree. I'm just talking with her about options.'

'I hope she figures out what she wants to do with herself,' Shakira said as she left Emily in the hallway with the clothes.

Once Agnes had a bath and her hair was dried, she looked like the fresh witch Emily knew. It was weird to see her in casual clothing, as she was always dress so provocatively, in sensual dresses that showed either a lot of leg or cleavage.

Agnes stayed with Emily until Kordell arrived at night to pick her up. Agnes was deeply shaken by Rodger's death. She would be staying with Kordell for a few days.

When Kordell picked up Agnes and took her back to his flat in Lewisham, Emily was alone with the cold realisation that the only other Destiny Walker she had ever known was now dead. She deeply hoped that Agnes would be able to help her, she couldn't bear to go down the deadly path that Rodger had experienced. She didn't want to suffer the way he had. She wanted to be happy.

Emily was deeply shaken but didn't show it to Shakira or Lisa. She didn't let them know anything about the supernatural world she belonged to and all the shit it brought with it.

***

Emily struggled to accept the news that Rodger had killed himself. Imagining the only other Destiny Walker she had ever met dead really freaked her out. She had never experienced someone dying firsthand. She may not have known Rodger well, yet she'd had a deep desire to help him.

A week had passed since his death. Emily had found it difficult to concentrate at university. Yet she had struggled through the week.

It was now Saturday, and Rafael was staying over in Shakira's room. Emily was happy that Shakira had a lovely boyfriend. Not only was he handsome but very polite and seemed good for Shakira. Her friend was easing up on her drug use and Emily felt this was because she had someone solid in her life.

Lisa and Aiden had gone to visit Lisa's parents in Hammersmith, where they were staying for the weekend. Emily enjoyed spending time with Shakira and her boyfriend. They ordered pizza and watched *The Lost Boys* on DVD.

At eight in the evening, Kordell visited Emily. He greeted Shakira and her boyfriend briefly. Emily noticed how his face fell and a distressed look consumed the handsome vampire's features.

When Emily was alone with Kordell in her room, he seated himself on the armchair she had recently acquired, which was by her bed. Emily sat on the bed and put on a DVD on her laptop.

'What are we watching tonight?' Kordell asked. Kordell was like a best friend to Emily.

'I was thinking we could watch *The Office*. I got the DVDs from a charity shop recently.'

Kordell agreed it was nice. He asked her which charity shop and she told him how it was Cancer Research in Lewisham town centre. Kordell and she would spend quality time together. He had been twenty-five years old when he was turned into a vampire and so his appearance didn't look out of place for him being her friend.

After the two watched one episode of the comedy show, Emily asked Kordell how Agnes was doing.

'She will recover from Rodger's death. She's a tough woman...' Kordell looked uncomfortable. 'I need to tell you something about Rafael and I know it's going to really upset you.'

'What?' Emily felt worried contemplating what Kordell could have to say about Shakira's boyfriend.

'He's not real.' Kordell looked sad as he spoke.

'What do you mean?'

'You must have accidently created him. I can feel that. He's a creation of your will.'

Emily absorbed the information. She felt like she was going to throw up.

'I know this is a lot to take in. Yet you need to break the will the same way you did when you made that guy Parker like you. You just need to imagine Rafael and then will him to stop being the illusion that he is.'

'Are you sure he's not real?' Emily said, feeling tears about to surface.

'I'm one hundred percent sure. He doesn't have any emotions or a soul. He is an illusion and he would attract dangerous supernatural beings towards your friend Shakira. They'd sense the magic surrounding her and him.'

'What do I need to do?'

Kordell instructed Emily to imagine Rafael's face, imagine the first time that Shakira met him when she was there, how Emily felt. She needed to imagine that the shards of reality that didn't exist in him were being blown away like sand in a desert.

Emily closed her eyes and thought of this. She felt the truth of Kordell's words, because as she imagined Rafael, she could sense he wasn't human and had no emotion. Something she wouldn't have known unless Kordell pointed it out.

She imagined Rafael fading away and turning back into the nothingness where he came from. She remembered his friend who he had come to the bar with, and knew how the band was a fabrication that would fade into memories too. They even had music on Spotify, yet it had all been an illusion created by Emily's unconscious will.

As she thought of the spell breaking and the truth of Rafael's illusion coming into place, she heard a sound in her mind like glass breaking on hardwood floor.

Kordell stayed with her till it was late at night. He assured her that Agnes would help her and that they would manage to bind her powers.

'I need to learn to manage my powers. I can't keep fucking up like this.'

'Agnes is going to help you. She has to.'

Emily could feel that Kordell was feeling sad for her. She could feel he was worried about her and that he was scared of how dangerous her powers could become.

At three in the morning, Kordell left the house and made his way back to his flat. When Emily was alone in her room, she wondered how Rafael would cease to be in Shakira's life.

Emily eventually fell asleep that morning around five. She had dreams of darkness and depression. Her dreams illustrated her subconsciouses terror at what she had become. Being a Destiny Walker was a true curse.

Emily awoke to Shakira entering her room. Her housemate didn't even knock. Shakira was crying.

'Rafael's left me. He took all his things in the night. He's deleted all his social media and just left me a note saying it's over. I thought everything was going so perfectly. I don't understand why he would do this.'

Emily did her best to comfort Shakira. Her friend cried as she sat on the bed with Emily. Emily could feel the deep sense of rejection and pain Shakira was experiencing. She could feel how Shakira had loved Rafael.

Chapter 14

Shakira was using drugs more heavily. Over the last month, she would use cocaine on a daily basis. Emily and Lisa talked amongst themselves about how they were worried about their friend. Shakira expressed how she was fine and doing well at work, yet Emily didn't believe that she was OK. She could sense that her friend was still devastated by Rafael dumping her the way he did. Yet Emily knew the truth about how she had accidently created Rafael and he had been nothing more than an illusion of love.

Emily was working on an essay on modern art for her studies in the living room. It was November and the weather outside was bleak. Emily's relationship with Dean was so romantic, and she imagined soon they would delve into the sexual side of dating. Emily wasn't too worried about this, because she knew that Dean regarded her with such affection and genuinely thought her beautiful.

As she typed the outline of her essay in the living room, Lisa and Aiden were cooking a vegan curry. Shakira was out at work.

Lisa and Aiden were laughing as they cooked together. Emily's mind was on Shakira and wanting her to be OK. She had no idea she had worked her will once more.

Lisa suddenly dropped the plate she was holding. It crashed on the floor, and she stepped away.

'What the actual fuck,' said Aiden. 'What the hell am I realising about you, Emily? Why am I seeing these images flash before my eyes and knowing that it's real?'

Emily instantly stopped what she was doing and felt a ping of terror run through her.

'I see it too, she's a Destiny Walker and Kordell's a vampire, that guy who always visits the house. He's an actual un-dead thing.' Lisa's voice was quiet yet there was force in her words.

'You've been hiding this world from us all,' Aiden said. 'You're an un-godly abomination.'

Emily felt sick and so scared to think that Aiden and Lisa now knew what she was. She didn't know what this would mean for her life here in the house. She was also scared for them, not knowing how they would react to their knowledge of her supernatural truth.

'Look,' Emily said, doing her best to compose herself, 'I'm going to bring Kordell round, he's going to have to compel you not to tell my secret.'

'What? No!' shouted Lisa.

'It's either that or I will you to keep the secret. That could go really wrong, so this is the way it has to be.'

Lisa and Aiden talked amongst themselves as they waited for Kordell to visit that night. When the vampire arrived, he looked at the couple with a sad expression.

'Knowing about this supernatural world is a burden. I'm sorry you won't be able to tell anyone else about it. Yet take solace in the fact that you will be able to talk amongst yourselves about these truths,' Kordell said.

Lisa and Aiden looked frightened as they held hands. Kordell first compelled Aiden, and Emily watched as the vampire worked his powers over the tall young man. Then it was Lisa's turn. Emily saw how her friend was shaking and crying as the vampire compelled her to keep Emily's secret for the rest of her life.

Lisa and Aiden wouldn't be able to tell anyone about anything regarding the supernatural world. It felt sad to Emily to know her power had cursed those around her once more. She had wanted to keep them safe from the secret.

'I saw everything in that realisation,' Lisa said. 'How this all began when a women crashed into you when we were going out. How you made Rafael and how he wasn't even a real person. I know it's not your fault, but I can never think of you the same way. You're no longer lovely, ditsy Emily, you're this cursed person who knows vampires and witches. You're a living nightmare.'

Emily knew that Lisa and Aiden wouldn't ever be able to tell her secret. She let them have some alone time. The couple looked shaken and like frightened mice.

In Emily's bedroom, she hugged Kordell and felt the tears flow from her eyes.

'I hate this life,' Emily cried.

'We're going to fix you, I promise.'

Kordell and Emily watched *Star Wars* in her room. The vampire told her how Agnes was close to finding a spell that could bind her powers. Emily felt hopeful knowing that Kordell would never lie about such a thing, yet her spirits were low this evening.

When it was nearing the end of the night, Kordell left the house. Emily saw that the light was still on in Lisa and Aiden's room, but she didn't dare knock on the door.

Shakira was home, yet she was in her room drinking and had brought home a random guy. Emily could hear them laughing. Emily felt worried for Shakira but was glad that she didn't know the truth about her identity. She couldn't imagine the horror her friend would experience knowing that Rafael hadn't been a real person. She knew that they had been sexually intimate, and she imagined how freaked Shakira would have been if she had been the one to find out the truth.

That night Emily cried herself to sleep. She felt a river of sorrow consume her. The curse of being a Destiny Walker was a black fog over her life which brought horror and confusion into her world.

She thought about how good her life would be without the supernatural. She was doing so well at university and things were going great with Dean. Yet she also had her secret life as a Destiny Walker which turned her normality into chaos.

Chapter 15

Emily had finished her second year at the University of Avenna. So had Lisa. Emily was sad about the events which had taken place over the last few months in the house. Lisa and Aiden had hardly spoken to her. When they had, she had felt the cold anger radiate from the couple who believed she was a curse. They were both frightened of her because of the fact that she had been able to create Rafael.

Shakira was no longer working at the pub in London, she had been fired after being caught doing drugs in the toilets. Yet she was starting to turn her life around now, a month later.

The group had all decided to go their separate ways. Lisa and Aiden were to move into a flat that Lisa's parents had purchased for her in Hammersmith. Emily didn't expect she would see Lisa again unless she bumped into her at university. It made Emily sad because Lisa had been one of her best friends.

Shakira was going to a rehab clinic in Spain and then she was going to travel. She had plans to go start university again after her travels.

As Shakira was packing the last of her things, Emily knocked on her door.

'It all ends tomorrow,' Shakira said. 'No more takeaways together and having drinks at the Fox and Ferkin. I'll miss this house.'

'I'll call you often,' Emily said as she watched her beautiful friend put the last of her clothes in a box.

'I'm so glad you've got Dean. He's been so good for you.' Shakira's eyes lit up. 'I'm excited about truly staying clean. It's been two weeks sober of drugs. I'm thinking of kicking the booze too.'

Emily and Shakira talked about their plans. Emily felt sad to leave all this behind.

Yet she was excited about the summer with Dean. They had rented out a room in a shared house in Beckton. The other students in the house were quiet. Emily was hopeful that moving in with Dean would be the right thing.

She was in a sexual relationship with him and the sex was good. She felt comfortable with him. At ease in her own body. When he said she was beautiful, she believed it.

As the residents of Grace Road packed their belongings, Emily was excited for the future. She had to believe Agnes would save her from more disasters. She didn't want to end up like Rodger, who had gone mad with the curse of the Destiny Walker.

Chapter 16

Days before Emily was to move into the shared house with Dean, Agnes had finally found a spell that would bind her powers. Emily arrived at the house nervous yet deeply excited.

Agnes greeted her with a calm smile. The beautiful witch invited her and Kordell into her lavish property. In the room where she cast spells, she opened a small metallic book.

She read the spell, which was in Greek. As she spoke the words, Emily began to shake and feel incredibly cold. Her body felt like it was being frozen from inside and then suddenly she heard the air around her pop. As she felt the temperature quickly come back to normal, she fell to the floor.

Kordell wrapped her in a blanket and Emily cried. She felt the magic freeze her curse into the core of her heart. She knew she could break the bond if she so chose, yet she knew she never would. Her powers were bound and only her choosing would unbreak that bind.

'You're free,' Agnes whispered.

'It's worked, I can feel it,' said Kordell.

'You're free, you're finally free of this nightmare,' Agnes said with tears of joy running down her face.

Agnes cooked Emily and herself a warm meal. Kordell simply drank black coffee in their company. Agnes spoke of all the things Emily could do with her life now she was free.

'I'll always be looking out for you, as will Kordell.'

Emily felt a sense of peace she hadn't known since before the strange woman had bumped into her just under a year ago. Life would never be the same. She was friends with a witch and a vampire. Yet she would never open up her curse, she just wanted to live a relatively normal life.

Chapter 17

Emily was at a place where life was the nearest to normality it would ever be. She was soon to be moving in with Dean; they were excited about the double bedroom they were renting in the shared house in Beckton.

Emily had learnt to harness her powers. She felt assured that the will she had invoked on herself was rock solid. She had hope that life would be good.

It was the summer before her third year at university. She could face the world with Kordell at her side.

Yet as he sat on the bench in the middle of the night, a strange feeling stirred in Emily, a sense of knowing something bad was soon to happen.

'You don't need me anymore,' Kordell said. 'You have Agnes and your power has been bound. You're going to get to live a relatively normal life.'

'Of course I need you, you've become my best friend in all of this.'

'Mine too. I never thought I'd share the company of a mortal in the way I have with you. You've been quite entertaining over this year. I'm happy that I was able to help you, I truly mean that.'

Emily looked at Kordell. His bleached blond hair and high cheekbones made him striking. Yet there was a quiet aura of misery in Kordell. She knew why; he hated that he had killed someone in the 1950s. It still haunted him as though it was today.

Emily wished she could say to him how it hadn't been his fault. His maker George had compelled him to do so. He'd had no choice, and yet the guilt had taken his life into a place of darkness. Kordell looked at vampires as despicable monsters who should be rid from the Earth. He didn't see immortality as a blessing but a great curse.

Kordell looked at her with a serious expression and she felt a sensation she remembered him invoking in her before, that wave of compulsion that felt like the ocean was roused in her.

As the vampire looked into her eyes and gripped her will, she noticed how he was crying.

'Emily, you are not going to stop me from doing what I will do today. You can either stay with me for the last night I have in this world or you can walk away, but you will not complain or try and stop me from doing this.'

Emily understood. She had no choice under the most intense compulsion Kordell had ever roused in her. She knew he planned to die by the sun and the thought of it brought tears to her own eyes.

'I understand. I will stay with you tonight,' Emily said, wishing she could use her powers over him to stop him. Yet his compulsion overrode any wish she could now make. She also knew doing such an act would endanger her stability with her powers and her curse.

Kordell sat with her on the bench. He talked about his childhood and how he had been from an affluent family who had not known he was gay. He expressed how no one really knew this, except the young man who he had been forced to kill because of his maker George.

Kordell described in detail how it hurt his soul so deeply to kill the young man who he had romantic feelings for. A man who he had shared a quiet kiss with days before being turned into a vampire.

'Even if it had been someone else, the act of murder destroyed my inner happiness,' Kordell said quietly. 'I am so grateful I was able to help you and Rodger. I feel it was something that will redeem me.'

'George was the true murderer, not you,' Emily said.

'Yes, I suppose you're right. Yet it doesn't stop the feelings of disgust, when I remember the thirst and how at the root of what I became, I enjoyed the kill. Vampires are addicted to bloodlust.'

'You've been such a good friend to me,' Emily said.

They watched the people walk by in Lewisham town centre, and soon they got off the bench and walked around until they were in the graveyard by the church, which was near Emily's old rented property on Grace Road.

'I have left my flat to you,' Kordell said. 'I got Agnes to make it so the deeds are in your name. You can sell it one day or perhaps rent it out. No other supernatural being apart from Agnes knows of its whereabouts.'

'All I can say is thank you so much for your last acts of kindness.' Emily felt sick with sorrow.

'I'd like you to read my diaries. They're in the living room.' Kordell handed her a key to the flat. It was a beautiful property. It was a one bedroom flat in the posh part of Lewisham.

Kordell told her how his diaries would explain a lot about the supernatural world. She would learn all that he knew on Werewolves, Fairies and true Psychics. Kordell expressed how he had loved their friendship.

Yet as the early morning hours crept in and the sun began to rise, Emily felt the sense of peace radiate off him. He was ready to die and believed that he would finally find peace.

As the sun began to burn his skin, as the first light of morning opened up, Kordell thought of the young man he had killed. His soul imagined that young man with pale skin and brown hair looking at him now and welcoming him to the other side.

Emily was there with him as the sun became fierce towards him. As the light of day directed its rays at his vampiric flesh, which melted and burnt in the light. Silver energy seemed to weave into the air around him. Kordell didn't scream, yet it was evident the sun was hurting him greatly.

When it was over and the light had burnt him into a mixture of fire that soon turned to ash, leaving black cinders as the remnants of her best friend, Emily fell to the floor crying.

No one but her was in the graveyard. She could feel Kordell's presence leaving this place. She could feel he was happy, and although her heart was broken she knew he had made the right decision for himself.

Emily looked down at the remains of Kordell, which simply looked like someone had burnt something. No supernatural evidence remained.

She walked to his flat and let herself in. She saw that there was a photograph of Kordell and herself on the mantlepiece in a silver frame. He had written a letter to her, stating how she was to call the flat home, yet if she wanted she could sell it.

Emily would keep the flat. She couldn't bring herself to clear it of the vampire's things. His designer clothes and remnants from the 1950s from when he had been alive.

She would visit the flat often. She didn't care about the money that a sale could generate. Kordell would be here for her, in the diaries he had left her.

Emily looked through his wardrobe; Christian Dior and Vivienne Westwood were evidently his favourite designers. He didn't have many possessions, yet she found that in the wardrobe, there were stacks of money.

On top of the stack of money, there was a little post-it note which read, *use this dosh wisely, my friend.*

Emily counted the money which was in stacks of five thousand. There must have been half a million there. She put one of the stashes of five-grand notes in her bag and decided she would deposit it into her bank. This would pay the rent on her room for the next two years.

Yet perhaps after university, she and Dean could move into Kordell's flat. She thought how the prospect would make Kordell happy. She imagined the future without her best friend.

If she had never met him who knew what a tragedy her life would have been. She thought of Rodger and how they had helped him so much. Yet Rodger had been a train wreck before meeting her and Kordell.

She locked up the flat and took the money to her local Santander branch in Beckton. There she deposited the five grand into her account. She would open a new account with another bank tomorrow and deposit the rest of the money.

When she got back to the shared room in Beckton, she felt so sad. Dean had not yet moved in and the room was just a double bed and her laptop and things. Emily wanted to tell Dean everything and she knew he would listen. He had accepted her supernatural world easily. He would be deeply sad to know Kordell was gone.

***

The next day Emily opened a NatWest account, and by the end of the week had just under half a million in the account. She wasn't planning to tell anyone about her newfound wealth. Not Dean or her parents. Yet she would tell Dean about the flat and how next year when university was over for herself they could move in, or perhaps wait until the following year when Dean had finished his bachelor's degree.

When Dean moved into the room, it soon felt coloured with his beautiful essence. He brought his gaming PC and his PlayStation 3.

Emily would always miss Kordell. Not a day would go by that she wouldn't think of her vampire best friend. Yet she was grateful that he had looked after her in the inheritance he had given her. She knew he was at peace, she just felt it so deeply in the core of her being.

Chapter 18

Emily never forgot Kordell. She always remembered him. Ten years had passed since she was cursed as a Destiny Walker. She was still in regular contact with Agnes.

She lost contact with Lisa and Aiden, yet Shakira was still friends with them. They were married and had two daughters.

Emily had married Dean, who knew the truth of her supernatural life. He had met Agnes, who had shown him visions of the realities Emily had experienced. He hadn't been afraid, which surprised her. He said he would always keep her secret. There was no vampire to compel him to do so. Kordell had been dead for ten years.

Emily had eventually moved into his one-bedroom flat in Lewisham once she had finished university. She had achieved a 2:1 in her fine art degree. A year later, Dean had got a first in his counselling degree. The couple were planning on one day having a child. They had recently rented out Kordell's house and bought a house in Devon with the money from the rent.

Dean worked as a counsellor for teenagers, while Emily worked as an art teacher. She was happy. Her life was marked by the supernatural yet she had experienced ten years of normality.

She was still in touch with Shakira, her closest friend in the world. She never told her the truth, fearing it would break the fabric of her good life. Shakira got her social work degree and now lived in Spain, where she helped people with drug problems.

This is the story of Emily and the people she met during her life in Grace Road, Lewisham. She was the girl they all knew, yet never truly knew because of her curse.